THE COST OF CARING

CAN A FRESH START ERASE THE PAST?

CARMEN KLASSEN

The Cost of Caring

By Carmen Klassen

ALSO BY CARMEN KLASSEN

SUCCESS ON HER TERMS

Book 1: Sweet, Smart, and Struggling

Book 2: The Cost of Caring

Book 3: Life Upcycled

Book 4: Heartwarming Designs

Book 5: A Roof Over Their Heads (Preorder)

* * *

NON FICTION

Love Your Clutter Away

Before Your Parents Move In

CONTENTS

CHAPTER 1

Lisa sat beside her mom in the front row of the funeral home chapel, still wearing her gray dress coat—she didn't plan on staying very long. She faced her dad's coffin with a strange mixture of distaste, anger, and sadness. The picture of him on the coffin was from his early twenties. Long before he met her mom and became saddled with a child he never wanted. Like someone she should have known, but never did.

They had waited an extra twenty minutes before starting the service in case anyone else showed up. There was nobody besides the two of them. Finally, Lisa leaned over to her mom, "Should the officiant start, Mom?"

Her mom looked at her in surprise. Maria was wearing a dark skirt with a cream top that Lisa helped her put on that morning. It was a shock to see how much arthritis had debilitated her in the past four years—she looked much older than forty-four. She supposed her dad had been the one to help her mom until now. But it was probably the only thing he had ever done for her. He liked his women quiet and obedient and hadn't let her or her mom have a say in anything. Maybe that was why Maria didn't realize it was up to her to begin the service. She turned and gave the officiant waiting at the corner of the stage an apologetic nod. He took her cue and stepped forward.

"We are gathered here to remember Robert Naylor, husband to Maria Naylor and father to Lisa Naylor…"

As the officiant's voice droned on, giving meaningless trivia about a man who had been nothing in his life except cheap and mean, Lisa's thoughts drifted back to the last time she was in the same town as her dad…

From her place on the stage, Lisa looked out on the sea of parents, friends, and family. At last, she had made it to her high school graduation. She knew her dad wouldn't come, but she had hoped her mom would stand up to him for once and come to support her. Obviously she had caved, again. That morning when she asked her mom one more time to come to her graduation, her dad had interrupted, "It's no big deal. Everyone graduates. You're nothing special, and your mom won't waste her time coming to see you."

She had looked at her mom, trying to communicate to her how important it was to have *somebody* at her graduation. But she refused to make eye contact. Now, Lisa would walk across the podium, accept the diploma that she had worked so hard to get, and then turn around and walk out of this town for good.

There was polite applause when Lisa went up to collect her diploma, but nobody really knew the girl walking across the stage. She had done her best to blend in at school. At 5'5 she wasn't tall or short, and in her 'uniform' of dark straight-leg jeans, plain black sneakers, and gray t-shirts and sweatshirts over her average-sized body, people seemed to look right through her. Her dark brown hair was in a single French braid, and if anyone had gotten a closer look, they would have seen sad brown eyes and a light coat of mascara—the only makeup she could put on that her dad didn't notice.

After trying to dodge all the proud families taking pictures of their children in caps and gowns, Lisa left her own cap and gown at the registration table and went to the café where she had worked and avoided her parents for the last two years. The owners were sad to see her go. She was the only employee who was willing to work evenings, weekends, and holidays, come in on a moment's notice, and do any job without complaining. Her last paycheck was waiting for her.

Mr. Shoud, her 10th grade accounting teacher, had helped her get the job, and then went with her to the bank to open her own account when she turned sixteen. He was one of the few people in her life she had asked for help. As an old timer in the town, he knew about her dad, and had encouraged Lisa to create her own future by getting a job and protecting her earnings. For two years she had lied to her dad every time she went to work, claiming she was 'hanging out'. He saw little value in her, and believed she was a waste of life, so it was easy to let him think she wasn't doing anything useful. The café she worked at served a trendy crowd who preferred organic, natural ingredients for their meals, and her dad had never gotten wind of his daughter's secret life.

She picked up her final paycheck, deposited it in her bank account, and withdrew enough cash for a bus ticket. The past year she had spent any free hours when she wasn't working or studying in the library at the public computers researching jobs in the city, and the cost of everything from bus tickets to rent. Her escape was a dream she clung to as she struggled alone to pass her classes and work as many hours as she could. She was as ready as she'd ever be.

Back at home, she went straight to her room. Nobody asked her how the ceremony had gone or congratulated her. Nobody even said hello. She quickly packed her work outfits, a few changes of clothes, a blanket, some toiletries, and a picture of her grandparents. It was a tight squeeze in her backpack, but she didn't want it to be obvious that she was leaving. Her dad's big plans for her involved getting a full-time job and paying him back for all the "years of bleeding me dry" that he claimed she owed him. She walked out of the house without saying goodbye and never looked back.

CHAPTER 2

Lisa was suddenly brought back to the present by her mom struggling to stand up. The service was over. She tucked her arm under her mom's and helped her get to her feet. It seemed like she was shorter than Lisa remembered, but she still wore her thin brown hair in a braid and her dark brown eyes still stood out against her pale cream skin. With Lisa's support, she walked to the coffin and stood there. "I don't know what I'll do without him" she whispered.

Lisa bit back a reply. This day changed nothing for her. Slowly her mom turned, and they walked out of the chapel. They had arranged a cremation which would take place after they left. Lisa supposed she'd have to come and pick up the ashes later. It would be tempting to dump them in the closest garbage can and be done with it.

When they arrived back home, Lisa was reluctant to come in. She had taken the bus straight from the city in the morning, arriving at the house in time to help her mom dress, and drive to the funeral chapel in her parent's car. She planned on a quick check on her mom, and then she'd be heading back to her room in the city. Work had offered her the week off upon hearing that her dad had passed away, but she didn't expect to need it.

"Do you have everything you need Mom? I want to catch the 5:30 bus back."

"You're leaving?"

"Well, yeah. I've got to get back to work… You'll be fine!"

"I don't know what to do. Your dad did everything. You have to take care of things now."

"Mom, you're a grown adult just like me. Now you've got the house and the car and dad's life insurance and whatever he left you."

"I don't think he left me anything. I don't know about any of that Lisa! You have to help me!" Maria looked on the verge of panicking, her eyes wide and filling with tears.

After being on her own for so many years, Lisa had forgotten how indecisive and meek her mom was. Bracing herself, she forced a smile on her face. "I can stay for a day or two and get everything figured out. How about we eat something, and then we can look through Dad's paperwork and see how you're set up. Does that sound good?"

Her mom smiled and rested her hand on Lisa's arm. "Thank you. I'm glad you're here."

Lisa couldn't find much food, so she heated up a can of tomato soup and toasted some stale bread that they ate before she went over to the desk where her dad had kept his papers. Hours later, Lisa couldn't find any evidence that he had made plans in case of his death. What she did find was a worrying number of bills that were past due, and three credit card statements that were over limit and past due. They were from a year ago, and she hoped he had paid them since. "I guess we should make an appointment at the bank Mom. Maybe he's got a safety deposit or something we don't know about. Did you get a death certificate from the funeral home? You may need that."

She called the bank, but they didn't have anything available until the next day. Now she just needed to pass the time for the rest of the day and night. "OK Mom, it looks like I have some time. What can I do here?"

"I don't know Lisa. Your dad would always know what to do."

Lisa was beyond frustrated with her mom's helplessness. Maybe she was just grieving, but she wouldn't survive a week if she didn't start making some decisions!

Thinking back, she struggled to remember the last time she had talked to her mom—really talked to her. Her dad had worked nights at a plant near the house, and even the quietest words during the day were enough to wake him up, angry, and yelling at everyone.

Until she was ten or eleven, Lisa remembered enjoying time with her mom when her dad was at work. But at some point that had changed. Then, even when he wasn't at home, during every conversation she tried to have with her mom, she always acted like her dad was still there. The phrase "Your dad wouldn't like that..." was one of the only things that ever came out of her mom's mouth.

Eventually Lisa quit talking to her mom. After leaving home she called once a year on her mom's birthday, but often even that conversation was ruined by him talking over her mom from across the room.

At least Maria had enough sense to keep Lisa's phone number and call her when her dad had collapsed at work. She wasn't even sure why she had come home for the funeral—she guessed that deep down she must still care about her mom.

Without knowing what her mom wanted now, and without anything else to do, Lisa went through his papers again to see if she could make sense of his finances. As a bookkeeper at least that was something she could do really well.

At suppertime she found her mom sitting on a chair looking out the front window. She wondered how long she had been there. "Mom? Are you hungry?"

"Oh, Lisa!" She seemed surprised to see her. "I'm very hungry. It's strange to not have your dad bellowing for his supper." A naughty smile tugged at the corners of her mouth. She would have never gotten away with a statement like that a few days ago.

"Let's go to the Hearthstone Café. They always have good food!"

"Eat out? No, we shouldn't."

"It's OK Mom, my treat. I'm not sure how you'd pay, anyway. Do you have a bank account in your name? I couldn't find anything in the paperwork."

"Oh no, your dad said I'd just waste all the money. We always did the shopping on his day off so he could keep an eye on me and pay for things. I don't know what I'll do now."

Lisa resisted the urge to roll her eyes, "Well, tomorrow we can open you an account when we go to the bank. Do you want to change before we go?"

"Oh no, your dad always said I should wear my outfits for a few days. I need his help to do the laundry now you know."

"No, I didn't know. Well if you want to change I can do laundry for you when we get back from supper." Her mom decided not to change. And since Lisa hadn't planned on staying for more than a few hours, she had nothing to change into. So they went dressed in their black and gray outfits.

At the café, her old employers were happy to see her. They had always been nice and were a good memory from Lisa's past. Her mom was shocked they knew her, and even more shocked to learn that her daughter had worked nearly full-time for them for two years before leaving home.

"How did you think I got the money to move out?"

"Your dad told me you probably stole it from people." She said it so matter-of-factly, Lisa could hardly speak.

"Did you believe him?"

"It was always better not to question him. If I tried to defend you, he would go on and on and made more accusations. That's what he did. But no, I didn't think you would have done that."

They ate their meal in relative silence after that. Lisa had no idea what was running through her mom's mind, but her own thoughts focused on how fast she could get her mom set up on her own so she could get back to her job. She had big dreams that were about to come true, and every day spent here instead of working and house-hunting was a day lost.

Sitting across from her mom it was tempting to relive all the hurt and rejection of her childhood. The sooner she could get back to her old life and put this behind her the better.

CHAPTER 3

The next morning the two women walked out of the bank into the bright Friday morning sun in a near state of shock. Lisa could feel her mom struggling to stand up, but she found herself almost unable to support her. They both collapsed onto the first bench they came to. Lisa leaned forward and put her face into her hands. It couldn't be true. Her dad spent his whole life being cheap and mean. He couldn't have possibly got his finances into such a desperate state.

But Lisa had seen the numbers. The bank officer became very sympathetic when he realized the ladies truly had no idea of their situation, but he couldn't take away the facts. Her dad had taken out a second mortgage on the home after maxing out all other credit options. Apparently, for years he left for work early every evening and spent a few hours at the casino before going to his job.

There was no protection for her mom. Everything was joint — without her knowledge. He set her up to take the fall for all his bad decisions. Lisa couldn't think of what to do next.

"That bastard," whispered her mom.

Lisa looked up, "What?"

"That bastard! When you left home, I desperately wanted to get a job. The house was so empty, and I had nothing to do. I could've worked at a store or something. But he refused. Said he made enough for us and I wasn't going to embarrass him by going out and looking for a job. I could've helped!"

"Mom, he would've just taken all your money and lost it too. That's why I never told you I had a job, because he would've taken all my paychecks."

"What do I do now?"

"I don't know Mom. Maybe bankruptcy? Then you might be able to get a small apartment or something? I don't know how that works."

"But the house is mine now, right?" For someone who hadn't had a penny to her name in decades, her mom struggled to understand her situation.

"Well, sort of. There are two mortgages on the house. Those are loans against the house's value. If we sold the house and everything in it, maybe we could clear most of the debts. And Dad might have a pension or something from work. He's been there all his life, so I'm sure there's something. But it might not be enough to live on. Do you still think you could get a job?"

"I'd love to work, but I'm limited now because of my arthritis. Sometimes I need an hour just to manage getting out of bed in the morning."

They sat there for a while silently. Then, very quietly her mom asked, "Could I live with you? I could help out a bit around the house. I really don't want to live alone."

"Mom, I rent a single room in a house full of college students. There's barely enough room for a bed and a dresser. And I share a bathroom with three other people. I've been saving every single penny so I could buy my own house one day. I couldn't have you live with me!" Lisa had to look away from her mom's pleading face. No way. She didn't owe her anything. It was her mom's fault she was in this situation. She wasn't going to throw away her own plans and life savings to fix something her dad had broken.

"Let's go home. Maybe something will work out." By the time they got home Lisa's mom was clearly in pain. She helped her into bed for a rest and went back to the living room. This problem wasn't going to fix itself in a day. She needed to take at least a full week off work. When she called, they were more than understanding. Lisa was entitled to up to two week's bereavement leave, and any holiday time she wanted to take. There would be some catching up to do when she got back, but it wasn't anything she couldn't handle.

Her freelance work was a different problem. At least she had brought her computer along, intending on working on the bus ride home. Even though Lisa had a good job as a bookkeeper, the salary wasn't enough to qualify for a mortgage. When she learned she could also work as a freelancer she jumped at the chance. Now she had ten clients that she did bookkeeping for remotely.

She had at least three hours of work due before tomorrow evening. But her parents didn't have internet.

Lisa did some cursory research using her phone's data but she'd have to find a place with good internet first thing in the morning so she could get her work done. At least the work was an escape from her current situation.

She shifted uncomfortably in the faded black jeans and plain gray t-shirt she put on that morning. Those clothes had been like a second skin to her just four years ago, but now they felt foreign—like they belonged to someone else. And without her hair styling products she had been reduced to putting her hair in a French braid that morning to keep it tidy. It felt like she was morphing back into the old version of herself and she didn't like it.

Lisa looked around her, trying to figure out what to do about her mom's situation. No matter what, she didn't want her mom stuck drowning in debt. Although her parent's house hadn't seen a single stroke of paint or an upgrade in at least twenty years, it had three bedrooms, a big yard, and was in a good school district. With a bit of luck, they could sell for a good price, but they still needed to sell off a lot of the contents too if her mom was going to get out of this debt free. Wherever she ended up, she wouldn't need a houseful of furniture.

In the garage, Lisa was surprised to find quite a collection of tools. She didn't remember her dad ever doing any work on the house, but he had spent some money on tools. It was just another thing he did for himself while denying his wife everything.

CHAPTER 4

The next morning Lisa was up early. It was nearly impossible to sleep in the house where she had felt so much pain as a teenager, and by 6:30 there was no point staying in bed. After finding another change of clothes that still fit (although they were nearly identical to what she wore the day before), she started cleaning out her room. The stuff there needed to go eventually, so she got to work. It was surprising how clean her room still was. For a space that hadn't been used in four years, she expected more dust. But everything was carefully cleaned, almost like it was ready for her, just in case she came back home.

An hour later, she had one box of things she wanted to keep—things like her high school accounting textbook which brought back fond memories, and some gifts her grandparents had given her when she was little. The rest was in bags to go to the thrift store or in the garbage can beside the house. She checked in on her mom, but she was still sleeping. Lisa finished by cleaning the light fixture and washing the windows. She'd vacuum later when her mom was up.

Still restless and anxious, Lisa went into the kitchen. The fridge and pantry were nearly bare. She wondered what her mom had eaten for the past week. For breakfast Lisa grabbed some crackers, one of the only things in the kitchen that she figured she could eat. It wasn't anything new to her.

In the house where she rented a room, the only safe place for food was locked in her room. Although the kitchen was communal with a rule that each person could label their food and leave it in there, her roommates were notorious for eating whatever they wanted, regardless of labels. Lisa kept crackers and apples in her room to eat in the morning before going to work.

Finally, Lisa couldn't wait any longer. She went to wake her mom up. "Mom? I need you to get up. Can you wake up? I have to go do some work."

Slowly she woke up, and the morning confusion cleared from her eyes when she saw her daughter. After helping her to the bathroom, Lisa gave her some privacy and went to get clean clothes out. She didn't care what the house 'rule' was, her mom would not wear clothes from the day before. Still waiting, she went to her dad's side of the bed and started looking through the drawers. She wasn't really looking for anything in particular, just taking advantage of the chance to do something she knew he wouldn't have allowed.

"What are you doing?" her mom wailed as she struggled to walk back from the bathroom.

"Going through Dad's drawers."

"You can't do that!"

"Really, Mom? Why not? What's going to happen?"

"Lisa! That's his stuff! It's private! You can't… you shouldn't…" Her mom slumped on the bed.

Lisa came and sat beside her. "He's gone Mom. And he doesn't have any power over you now. Or me."

"I did try to reason with him at first. To be strong." Tears filled Maria's eyes. It was the first time Lisa had seen her cry. "I wanted things to be better for you. But every time I tried to speak out for you it made him angrier. It was just safer to do what he said. I don't know how to do anything else."

"You're going to have to. You're still alive, and you've got a lot of good living ahead of you if you want."

"What about you? Do you have a good life?" She seemed to be trying to shift the conversation away from herself.

Lisa sighed. She was about to really start her good life when her dad's death had wrecked everything. "Yeah, Mom. I have a good life."

"Will you tell me about it?"

"I have to go find an internet signal and get some work done now. How about we talk more later? I'll tell you all about my life."

"That would be nice. I'll wait for you in the living room."

Lisa looked at her, thinking she was joking. But she seemed completely sincere. Was that all she did every day? Sit in the living room and wait for someone to come home? The idea seemed too horrible to bear. She needed to give her something to do.

"Mom, do you know if Dad kept paperwork anywhere else?"

"Well sure, he used to pack it into boxes and put it in the basement."

"OK. How about this. Let's get you dressed and set up in the living room. And then I'll bring up some of those boxes and you can look through them while I'm out. I need you to find any important papers and put the rest in a pile for recycling."

"Oh, I couldn't do that! I don't know anything about all that stuff!"

Again, Lisa was amazed at how helpless her mom thought she was. "Can you read?"

"Of course I can!"

"Good! Just read the papers, and anything you think is important put aside. You *can* do it, and it will make it a lot easier for me."

"Well, I'll try." And with that feeble commitment, Lisa helped her get dressed and then have some breakfast.

It wasn't hard to find the boxes and Lisa brought up more than enough to keep her mom busy for a few hours. She set her up on the couch and put the boxes within easy reach. "I'll see you in a few hours then Mom. Bye!"

"Bye! Don't be too long!"

Lisa decided to go back to the café. She figured it would have the most reliable Wi-Fi and there should be a free table during the slower hours before lunch. As always, the routines of numbers, balances, and spreadsheets calmed Lisa. She loved math and numbers. They never lied. If there was an error, it was a human one and could be fixed. Not like life, which was confusing and hard to fix.

By the time she caught up and sent off invoices for her work, she was feeling better. After a quick stop at the discount grocery store to buy a few days' worth of simple meals, she headed back home. It *was* a luxury to use her parents' car. In the city she relied on public transportation, and while it was cheaper than a car, it wasn't exactly convenient.

Back at home she was pleased to see that her mom had made excellent progress on the boxes of paperwork. Two of them were empty, the recycling bag was nearly full, and there was a small pile on the side table.

"Oh hi! That was quick!"

"I was gone for almost three hours!"

"Really? I didn't realize… the time went by so fast!"

"So, how did you do?"

"Well, it was mostly old bills and bank statements. Those didn't seem very important. But I did find a few papers I think we should keep. There are some car insurance papers, and the receipt for the new furnace we put in a few years ago. Your father sure was mad about that! And look here, is that a life insurance policy?"

Lisa looked over the papers. She didn't recognize the company name, but it certainly looked like a proper policy. It was for $10,000 and had been taken out in 2004. "Mom, did you find any current bank statements? We should try to see if he kept this policy up. It would have renewed in February of each year."

After a bit of shuffling, they confirmed he had made a payment on the policy every year. Lisa brought over the house phone and dialed for her mom so she could ask about the policy. Twenty minutes on hold, and just a few minutes of talking confirmed that the policy was still valid, and they just needed the death certificate and proof of Maria's identity to release the policy.

"Well Mom, I'd say you did pretty good! How often do you make $10,000 in a few hours?"

"Really? That money's really mine?"

"Sure! Just like all the debts are really yours too!"

"Oh, I had forgotten about that. What do we do now?"

"Let me take all this recycling out to the can and clean up here, and then have lunch and chat."

CHAPTER 5

Over a lunch of chicken wraps and salad, Lisa laid out her plan. It was clear to her now that her mom was in no position to live on her own. Even with the money from the policy, she needed to have someone around to keep an eye on her, at least until she learned how to take care of herself without needing to be told what to do.

Even though Lisa still struggled with resentment over the past, she didn't actually want to abandon her mom. There was something there—a connection, perhaps—that hadn't gone away. Whatever it was she wanted to build on it, not walk away from it.

Somehow, while she was focusing on her work that morning she had decided to take care of her mom. She didn't want to be cold and mean to her own family. That meant agreeing to be there for her from now on. As soon as she came to that decision she felt something inside her heart soften—even while her brain was worrying about how it would all work out, and what she would have to sacrifice.

"So, like I told you, I rent a single room in a house. I have a good job working as a bookkeeper, and I spend the evenings doing free-lance work. I'm almost ready to buy my own house. But for now, that can wait. As far as this place here goes, I think you should sell pretty much everything to pay off dad's debts. After that, I can find a two bedroom apartment to rent and I'd like you to come live with me."

It was the longest uninterrupted talk Lisa could remember sharing with her mom. B

ut Maria slowly kept eating her food, not even acknowledging what she had heard. When Lisa was ready to walk away and forget about the whole thing, her mom finally spoke.

"Why?"

"What do you mean?"

"I've barely talked to you for years. I don't even know you. I didn't go to your graduation. Why do you want me to live with you?"

Lisa was surprised to see her mom's eyes glistening. She reached over and placed her hand gently on her arm. "Because it feels right. And because maybe it will give us a chance to get to know each other. And I think it might be nice for you to not be alone all the time."

"I'd like that too. You can have that $10,000 insurance thing."

"There might not be much left of that money after all the bills are paid. But if there is, you need to keep it."

"I wouldn't know what to do with it. I've never had any money."

"That's why you need it. Every woman needs to have her own money, including you. But in the meantime, I need your permission to sell the house and the stuff in it. It *is* yours, and the final decision is up to you."

"I've always hated this house. Sell it!"

"What?"

"This house was your dad's parents', and they were terrible people. I didn't want to move here when they died, but he insisted. I can't wait to leave it!"

Armed with this new information, Lisa was more convinced than ever to put her savings plan aside for the moment and just focus on moving her mom into the city. She was used to big challenges, and even though this one was different, she could handle it. Although her first thought had been to just leave everything and get back to the life she loved in the city, she knew now she couldn't just walk away from her mom.

They spent the rest of the day sorting through household items, choosing to keep useful things, and putting the rest aside to be donated. Lisa took one break to go to the grocery store and filled her car with empty boxes while her mom rested. Aside from that, they only took a quick break for supper. By the time Maria was obviously done for the day they had sorted through the front hall closet, the kitchen, the dining room and living room, and the master bedroom. Through all of that, Lisa was amazed to not find a single sentimental thing her mom wanted to keep.

In the morning Lisa brought up the rest of the boxes of paperwork from the basement, and everything else she could fit in the living room. Her mom was quite worn out from her busy day prior, and Lisa encouraged her to just go through a few boxes, and then rest again. She had her own busy day planned. After getting her free-lance work done at the café, she'd drive the car into the city and try to find an apartment she could rent right away. If she was successful, she'd cancel the room she was renting for the end of the month. At least it was on a month-to-month lease so there would be no penalty for canceling.

Just after eight pm, Lisa drove back into the driveway. She sat and looked at the house for a minute before getting out. It would be nice if someone could buy it and turn it into a happy home. Going inside with a backpack that had some changes of clothes and toiletries in it, she was surprised to find that her mom had gone through almost all the boxes. And she finally found some things she wanted to keep for sentimental reasons: A little outfit Lisa had worn as a baby and some pictures of Lisa as a baby as well as pictures of her mom's parents, and even her mom as a baby. The rest of the stuff was either garbage or donations.

They had a late supper while Lisa talked about her day. She managed to find a two-bedroom apartment that was on the ground floor and looked to be accessible. It was a bit further from Lisa's work, but at least there was a bus stop nearby. Lisa had signed a six-month lease and rented a parking space so they could keep the car. They could move in right away. Her savings account was $2,500 less after paying for the damage deposit and first month's rent, but she didn't tell that part.

While Lisa cleaned up supper, her mom spoke up. "Could you help me to bed, and then maybe we could chat a bit? It takes me a long time to fall asleep, but I just can't sit anymore today."

Lisa agreed, and helped her with the bedtime routine. The two days of activity had taken quite a toll, and she was clearly in a great deal of pain. When she was finally settled in bed, Lisa felt a bit unsure what to do next. She had never been allowed in her parent's room as a child.

"Here, come sit beside me. I want to know how you got set to buy a house. You sure didn't learn about money from me!"

Lisa tried to ignore the fact that she was sitting where her dad used to sleep, and told her mom everything she had been holding to herself since she left home...

CHAPTER 6

Eighteen year old Lisa sat at the bus station overwhelmed with emotions. Terrified that her dad might somehow find out where she was and make her come home. Excited that she made it this far and was starting a life where she could do what she wanted. Worried that she might not find a place to stay that night and that she'd end up on a park bench, or worse.

When the bus finally came, she nearly ran to it and took the first seat in the front. Hugging her belongings to her, she tried not to think of all the other students in her graduating class who were celebrating with their families before attending the after-grad dinner and party at their town's nicest hotel.

She wondered if she should have avoided the whole ceremony and left town in the morning. It would have saved her the $35 fee for the cap and gown rental and given her more time to find a place in the city before nighttime. But she had hoped that her mom would come, and be proud of her, and maybe even ask how she had gotten the money to pay for everything. There were so many times when she was tempted to tell her mom everything—about working, and saving, and her dream to live on her own and one day buy a house.

But in the end, she kept it all from her mom, out of fear her dad would find out.

The café owners thought it strange when sixteen year old Lisa applied for the part-time dishwasher job and practically begged them to let her use their address for her mail. But she had proven to be a hard worker who never complained, and soon they got used to the quiet girl whose cell phone bill and tax documents came to the café mailbox. She became their best worker, able to cover wherever they needed her.

Now Lisa hoped that her experience in the kitchen and serving in the front of the café, along with the glowing reference her boss had given her would help her get a job as soon as possible.

Getting off the bus in the city, Lisa tried to pretend she knew what she was doing. She had never been more than half an hour away from home and the temptation to just stand and stare at all the busy-ness was almost too much to resist. All of her dreams about the city hadn't taken into account how overwhelming it would feel when she got there.

Adjusting her backpack and checking that her purse was secure across her shoulder, she walked into the bus station to get directions. The line up to buy tickets was too long to wait in, so Lisa looked around until she saw an older man who was well-dressed. He seemed surprised when she asked where the nearest library was but gave her easy to follow directions. It was only a short walk from the bus station.

With her one hour of free internet and access to a computer, she got to work. Her first goal was to find a room to rent that was near a bus or train station. The options were overwhelming. Her first search turned up over a thousand ads. Many of them asked for references and proof of employment, so after losing almost half an hour of time searching, she had the idea to look for 'student' room for rent. That narrowed it down enough for her to print up two sheets of options just before her time ran out.

There was a little coffee shop attached to the library where Lisa bought an overpriced sandwich and a bottle of water and then started making calls. Soon she had three people lined up who could show her places right away. Unsure about taking city buses and how long it might take to get to each place, Lisa stopped at a bank machine to withdraw more cash and then waved down a taxi. She had only seen people take taxis on TV shows and hoped that it was the same in real life.

The taxi driver was helpful, and after looking at her list of places determined the best route to see all three. He asked her twice if she could afford to pay him for the whole route but agreed to wait at each place. She figured it wouldn't take long to walk in and look at a room.

The first and second places were terrible. At the first, the garbage piled outside was an immediate turn-off. As soon as she realized the bedroom didn't even have a lock on the door, she quickly said no thank you, and left.

The second place was slightly better, but there was a strange smell to the entire place that she didn't think she'd ever get used to. The third place was the most expensive at $500 per month, but the house was clean, and the room had a lock. The landlord assured her there was a bus stop just a few minutes' walk away and claimed it was a good place for quiet students. He would let her have the room right away if she paid cash.

Back at the taxi, Lisa paid the driver $50 for the $46.70 fare. Then she used the landlord's directions to walk to the bank that was a few blocks away and withdraw $750 to pay for the damage deposit and half a month's rent. She had no idea if she was doing the right thing or not. She traded the handful of cash for a key to the front door, a key to the bedroom, and a very small list of house rules. Lisa learned later that the landlord never signed leases with any of his student tenants, so he could kick them out immediately if they didn't pay their rent on time.

Sitting on the bed in her new room with the door shut and locked,

Lisa felt very small and lost. And hungry. She left her backpack in the empty room, carefully locked the door, and walked back to the retail area where she had withdrawn cash earlier. At McDonald's with her meal in front of her she spontaneously took out her phone and called home. Relieved to hear her mom answer, she told her that she had moved out and wouldn't be coming back. Wanting to tell her everything, she started to talk, and then heard her dad in the background demanding to speak to her. She hung up before he could.

There was no one at the house when she returned, so after using the bathroom and making sure all the doors were locked, she went into her room for the longest night of her life. She had nothing. Not even a pillow or a sheet. At least she had brought a blanket. She plugged in her phone and set it and the photo of her grandparents on top of her backpack beside the bed. Then she lay there for hours, hearing every noise in a strange house and a strange neighborhood.

Lisa woke up the next morning freezing cold, stiff, and uncomfortable after sleeping wrapped up in a single blanket without a pillow. She went to have a hot shower, only to realize she didn't have a towel, or any toiletries besides toothpaste and deodorant. Doing her best to look presentable, she put her long dark hair into a French braid and pulled on her nicest pair of black jeans and a light blue t-shirt that had the café's logo on it. It was the nicest of her shirts. She unpacked the rest of her things onto her bed, and then grabbed her resume in a folder.

There didn't seem to be anyone else living in the house, although one of the other bedroom doors was closed. The other two were open and bare except for beds. She needed to find a place to photocopy her resume, find a job, and then buy some basics. There was no way she was spending another night sleeping on a bare mattress without a pillow.

Her first stop was the retail area closest to the house. After photocopying her resume at the drug store, she made her way through the stores. A little gift shop was advertising for help, and Lisa also left her resume at all the fast food restaurants. What she really wanted was somewhere she could make tips, but a job at McDonald's was better than no job at all.

It was nice that a branch of her bank was there, and she went in to get her address changed on her account and see about ordering checks. The landlord's only hesitation in renting to her was her inability to give him postdated checks for the rent, although he insisted on cash upfront for the damage deposit. She promised to have a check for him by the first of July.

Lisa had already learned that it worked well to pretend she was confident and capable in front of people her age and bosses, and to ask for help and advice from almost everyone else. At the bank, she explained to the teller that she was on her own for the first time and didn't know what to do about paying rent and bills. The teller offered to see if one of the account assistants was free to go over things with Lisa.

Fifteen minutes later, Lisa had enjoyed a free coffee and was sitting in front of a kind-looking older lady. She was very helpful, explaining that Lisa could get up to six checks printed for free at a time, instead of having to order the minimum two hundred. She also switched Lisa from a youth account with limited choices to a proper checking account where Lisa wouldn't have to pay to use her debit card or pay bills. Finally, she recommended Lisa get a small secured credit card so she could start building her credit.

All the credit information was new to Lisa, and she was grateful the lady took time to explain it, and then re-explain it when Lisa asked questions. She understood the numbers and interest charges easily, but the concept of leaving money that the bank could access to pay her bill took a while longer. When she felt she understood it, she agreed to a card with a $200 limit and filled out the application form.

Just before leaving the lady asked if Lisa was familiar with online banking. She admitted she only used the library computers to go online. The lady seemed surprised that Lisa didn't have her own computer, but suggested she consider online banking only when she could access secure internet in a private place.

When she left, she had her six free checks, and could expect her new credit card in the mail sometime next week. Being able to receive mail at her home was a novelty for Lisa and made her grateful she found something so quickly, even if it didn't have sheets or pillows.

Worried that she needed to hand out more resumes, Lisa went to the bus stop near her house so she could head downtown. She didn't know how to use the bus, but there were a few seniors waiting, so she asked them for help. One lady suggested she get a monthly pass if she would be using the bus every day. The $99 sounded like a lot of money, but at $3.50 each way, it would be cheaper to get a monthly pass in July, especially if she found more than one job like she was hoping.

Thanking them for their help, Lisa boarded the next bus for the city center.

Downtown, Lisa handed out another ten resumes to places advertising help wanted and then found herself by the library. She took advantage of the hour of free internet to look up jobs. It was nice that she could answer her cell phone whenever someone called about a job. Because her parents hadn't known she had a job or a phone, she had been careful to keep it turned off whenever she was at home.

After buying a hotdog from a street vendor, Lisa was ready to go home. All she needed was a store where she could buy some much-needed things for her room. She tried to talk to a few older people to ask them where she could buy things, but everyone downtown seemed a lot more suspicious.

As a last resort, she turned back to the library thinking she could try and find a city map or a newspaper with ads that would give her a clue about where to go. But she realized the librarian might be a better resource. She was right. Armed with a few store names, and a hand-drawn map, Lisa headed out for her first visit to a big box home store.

She spent nearly an hour looking at everything before making some decisions. Mostly she based it on price, since she didn't know how else to decide. When she walked out of the store, she had a pillow, a sheet set, a warm blanket, a towel and face cloth, some toiletries, and four collapsible baskets that claimed to be stackable. Then she followed the librarian's map in reverse until she got back to where the bus dropped her off earlier in the day. Crossing the street, she walked another block before finding the bus stop heading back home. Almost immediately the bus with the right number arrived, and she paid the fare before finding a seat near the front of the bus. She wanted to see the neighborhood coming up, so she didn't miss her stop.

When she got off the bus at the right stop Lisa felt a small surge of confidence. She had successfully navigated public transportation for the first time! Now all she needed was a job.

CHAPTER 7

Lisa was quite happy to set up her room with her new purchases. It made all the difference to have the bed made, and while the stacking baskets weren't very sturdy, they gave her a place to put her few belongings and rest her phone on, instead of on her bed or backpack. She forgot to buy hangers to hang up the work clothes she would hopefully need soon, so she laid out the black pants and white blouses flat on the floor.

Feeling rather proud of herself, she went to check out the grocery store nearby to get some things she could eat at home. If she could get a job waitressing, then she would eat at work as much as possible, which would save money.

The grocery store was almost as overwhelming as the home store. The only times she bought groceries before it was from a strict list her Dad had given her. She never had choices, just the instruction not to 'screw it up'.

When she got back to the house, she was shocked to find a guy sitting at the table in the kitchen. He looked about twenty years old, with dark hair nearly reaching his heavy eyebrows, the beginnings of a beard, sad looking eyes, and a slightly hunched posture.

"Oh, um hi. I'm Lisa."

"Chad. How's it going?"

"Good, I guess. I didn't know if anyone else lived here. Sorry. Well, um, nice to meet you." She turned with her bag of groceries and started to put the cheese and yogurt in the fridge.

"You won't want to do that in a few months."

"Sorry? What do you mean?"

"When the other students come back. You won't want to put any decent food in there. They'll just take it. Trust me."

"OK...Is it safe for now?"

"Yeah, I don't eat here. Wanna go get Chinese?"

And with that, Lisa and Chad became friends. Later on, she'd look back at the summer with a mixture of happy memories and a few regrets. Chad turned out to be great fun when he wasn't in a surly mood. He had Lisa going all over the city with him, to movies, restaurants, concerts, and lots of shopping. It was everything she imagined having a best friend could be—without worrying about him doing something stupid like going to her house and asking her Dad if she was still at work.

That had taken some fast lies to cover up! A new girl in Lisa's high school English class had befriended her, and they started to hang out at lunch. Without a thought Lisa told her where she lived when they were comparing how far they walked to places like school and work. Shortly after, the girl decided to visit Lisa at her house and nearly exposed all of Lisa's secrets. After that Lisa stayed away from friends for the rest of high school.

Now, she could go where she wanted, when she wanted, and with anyone she wanted, and she loved it. Chad worked at a restaurant a few blocks away, and soon Lisa was working there too. Whenever they weren't working they were out doing something. Lisa was often tired, but never bored. She learned from Chad how to master public transit, sneak in a double feature at the movies, and try all kinds of foods that she wouldn't have tried on her own.

Everything changed the week before university started. Chad quit work to focus on school, telling Lisa that he only worked in the summer to have extra cash. His parents covered all his expenses when he was in school. Lisa, on the other hand, had blown through the savings she had worked so hard for during high school, and wouldn't be getting any help from her parents even if she did go back to school one day.

And the house filled up with students. They all seemed nice. Jennifer and Colette shared one of the rooms and were both in their second year of nursing school. Mark rented the last room and was taking some sort of sciences. With the house no longer feeling like it was just for her and Chad, and with everyone busy at school most days, Lisa was forced to stop and take a look at her life.

She had enjoyed a whole summer of not having to hide from her dad or be disappointed by her mom. But other than that, she only had a part-time waitressing job that just barely covered her monthly expenses. And all she had to show for her empty savings account were some new clothes and a good idea of which restaurants in the city were the best for ethnic food. She wanted more out of life, but she didn't exactly know *what* she wanted, or how to get it.

As one of the non-students working at the restaurant, she began to take more day shifts. The tips weren't as good, but the hours were consistent, and she enjoyed getting to know the regulars. Once the manager knew he could rely on her, he gave her more responsibility —without more pay of course. But she drew the line when he tried to make her shift supervisor. There was no way she would deal with customer complaints and other servers not showing up for work.

The thing she enjoyed the most was cashing out at the end of the shift and reconciling all the receipts. It was often a challenge when things didn't add up, and most of the time she could figure out where the errors were and fix them.

In October, things changed for Lisa again. The manager caught her at the end of her shift and asked if she would stay a bit later to show everything to the new bookkeeper. By now, Lisa knew the cash and payment system better than him. He took her to the office and introduced her to Janet Daniels before quickly leaving.

Janet was a tiny lady, somewhere between forty and fifty years old, with clear-framed glasses, straight blond hair styled into a tidy bob, and dressed in a soft gray suit with a white blouse. In a matter of minutes, Lisa knew she had found a kindred heart who loved numbers and columns as much as she did. Janet hadn't done bookkeeping for a restaurant before, but she quickly caught on to the system they were using, and the challenges that came from servers always in and out of the tills taking payments.

Once Janet had all the information she needed, she put down her pencil and looked straight at Lisa. "Are you in school?"

Lisa had a hard time looking away from Janet's dark brown, piercing eyes. "Um, no. I work here almost full-time though."

"You're quick with numbers and you could do well with some book-keeping training. I suggest you consider it."

"Oh, well OK. I guess numbers are kinda my thing. I was the only one at my school who took accounting classes because I wanted to, not because I needed the easy math class. But I'm not very good at everything else."

"Most colleges just make high school graduation the pre-requisite for bookkeeping classes. I presume you graduated?" Janet talked like she wrote down numbers. Quick, sharp, and absolutely certain about everything she did. Lisa didn't know whether to feel impressed or intimidated.

"Yeah…"

"And do you have the resources to pay for classes?"

"Oh, no, I couldn't do that. I just barely make enough here to pay my bills."

"Well then, I guess you have your work cut out for you. If you're still here next month when I come for the receipts, I'll ask for an update."

She turned and placed the receipts and paperwork into a file folder labeled with the restaurant's name, and then put the folder into a black leather briefcase. Lisa got a glimpse of five or six other folders, all with business names on them before Janet closed the case, put on her jacket, and walked briskly out the door.

Lisa sat down on the newly vacated chair. Her favorite times at work were when she sat at this desk and reconciled the day's receipts. It would be neat to do that full-time. Heck, it would be neat to call herself a bookkeeper and not a server. But if she needed to take any English classes she'd be sunk. It took her forever to read anything, and she wasn't good at writing, either.

Finally, she stood up and left. Since it was Thursday, the library would be open late—she might as well see what a bookkeeping course involved. She got on the next bus downtown. It was weird to think that the last time she was on a bus alone she was asking about where to buy blankets and towels. That seemed like forever ago.

All the computers were already in use, so she went to the reference desk to see if they had any catalogs from the community colleges in the area. As usual, the man at the desk was more than helpful. He got out the current brochure and helped Lisa find the right section. She found a seat nearby and slowly read through the description. There were a lot of terms she didn't know, but things like accounts receivable and payable she had already learned a little in high school.

Going back to the counter, she asked if he knew how to apply. She felt a little silly when he pointed out the website at the top of each page, but he seemed understanding. He wrote down the website and the program on a piece of paper and pointed out a computer station that had just opened up.

Once she was on her own, Lisa struggled to find the right information on the website. She wanted to know what time the classes were, and how much they cost, but the pages had so much text on them she couldn't find what she was looking for. Finally, she picked up her phone and called the contact number at the bottom of the website.

The lady who answered offered to book Lisa into an introductory session coming up in a few weeks. Then Lisa could hear more, get a tour of the campus, and have questions answered by someone from their accounting department. Lisa carefully added the information into the calendar on her phone, and double checked everything before hanging up.

As she rode the bus home, she realized nothing would change in her life unless she got more work. Even if she didn't take any courses, she wasn't exactly making progress at her job. And with the money going out as fast as she earned it, she'd never be able to afford a place of her own. She needed to figure something out, soon.

CHAPTER 8

One month later, Lisa was ready for Janet when she arrived. All the receipts were carefully organized the way she saw Janet do it, and she was proud to have an update on her own situation ready for her.

Janet checked everything over and filed the receipts and summaries in her briefcase. Then, she looked straight at Lisa. "Alright, you have something to tell me. Go ahead."

This time it felt easier to return Janet's gaze. "I've decided to start taking bookkeeping courses. I went to an open house at the City Community College, got lots of information, and paid the $25 deposit to reserve a spot for the Intro to Bookkeeping class that starts in January. I've been applying for part-time jobs so I can pay for the course, but even if I don't find something, I should make enough extra tips over Christmas to pay for it."

After a long pause, Janet smiled. "I thought you had a spark in you. I'm glad to see I was right. What kind of part-time job would you like?"

"Oh, I'll do pretty much anything. As long as I can be shown how to do something, I can do it. Nothing that needs lots of reading though."

Janet took a business card from the side pocket of her briefcase and handed it to her. "This is where I have my office, and I own the building. Our janitor is retiring soon, and I need a replacement. It's hard work, but it pays well, and you leave when the job is done every night so the faster you work the sooner you leave. If you can come by between four and five anytime this week, you can shadow Manuel and see if you want the job."

Lisa barely had time to say thank you before Janet was up and out the door with her jacket and briefcase. She was a strange lady, that's for sure. But Lisa felt like she wouldn't say anything she didn't mean, or anything more than what she needed to say. And she really wanted to impress Janet.

It wasn't until she was walking home that she remembered that Janet said she owned the whole building. That was cool! How did a lady who didn't seem like she was married get enough money to buy an office building? Maybe she had rich parents or something. Lisa had learned at the college open house that bookkeepers could make between $25,000 and $50,000 per year, but she didn't think that was enough to buy an office building.

The next day Lisa hurried home from her shift so she could change out of her black pants and white dress shirt into jeans and a t-shirt and go to meet Manuel. She'd have to take a different bus, and it would be tight to get there by four.

Hart Professional Center was nicer than she expected. It was in an area near downtown, had underground parking, and was three stories tall. Lisa wondered how one person could keep it all clean. She stopped at the front desk and asked for Manuel. Soon a man came out to meet her. He was a lot younger than she thought someone about to retire should be. With a firm handshake, he asked her if she could do heavy work. But before she could answer, he added, "If Janet thinks you can, then you'll be fine. Come this way."

Manuel explained that there was a day time housekeeper who worked four hours a day and did the light cleaning. Janet had created the position for her. She did the windows, the dusting, and kept the bathrooms and supply room tidy and stocked. Once people began to leave between four and five, Manuel took over. The top floor was occupied by a medical research facility whose employees started early and were always out the door by four pm. That was the first floor to start cleaning: garbage cans needed to be emptied, floors vacuumed, and the bathrooms cleaned. Manuel said he could do it in an hour and a half if there were no major messes.

The next two floors were similar, and the tiled front entrance on the ground floor needed mopping every night before she left. Manuel said he was usually done by ten pm. He finished showing Lisa around the building, and then took her back to Janet's office, which was on the second floor. The sign on the door said Bookkeeping Services, and inside there was a small reception area, and doors leading to two offices. Janet's office door was open, and she appeared to be waiting for them.

"Thank you, Manuel. I hope you have a good night." Manuel said goodbye to both women and left.

"Well Lisa, you have an idea of what the job involves now. If you're taking night classes, you can work your schedule around your classes as long as the building is cleaned by midnight. This is a contract job, which means you are paid a flat rate, and you're responsible for paying your own taxes and any other financial obligations. I'm happy to help with filing taxes the first year, but I'm sure you'll be well able to do that all yourself in subsequent years. The rate is $600 weekly, regardless of holidays. You receive one week of training from Manuel at the end of the month and then you're on your own. I'll pay $500 for the training week. Would you like the job?"

Lisa sat looking at Janet and tried to make her brain work faster. Yes, of course she wanted the job! By why was this lady putting so much trust in her and giving her so much responsibility? She decided it didn't really matter. This job seemed to be the chance she was looking for and she was going to go for it.

"Yes, I'd like the job. Thank you so much!" Janet had a contract already prepared. She instructed Lisa to take it home and read it before bringing it back at the end of the week to finalize everything.

"If you don't understand anything in the contract, you can take it to the drop-in legal aid clinic at the courthouse. They'll review it with you at no charge."

CHAPTER 9

Lisa sat on the bus, slowly reading over the contract. There were a few words she didn't understand, so when she got home, she asked Chad if he could explain it. He thought she was crazy for taking on another job but did help her understand the contract. There was nothing in it that worried her, but she was curious what the Legal Aid Center would say.

It was two days before she had the chance to leave work early enough to get to the Legal Aid Center before it closed. After explaining the limitations of the advice they gave, a law student reviewed the contract with Lisa. She was grateful to Chad for helping her understand it so could keep up with the law student's fast talking. The only recommendation the lady gave her was to take out personal liability insurance, in case she really screwed something up. While the building offered coverage, it didn't include 'willful or gross negligence'.

On Friday Lisa was back in Janet's office ready to sign her first contract. Janet congratulated her on checking out the contract and following up on her concern about liability. Yes, she could recommend an insurance company. They both signed two copies of the contract, and Lisa felt grown-up for the first time in her life.

Holding the papers in her hand, she hesitated for a second, before asking Janet how she bought an entire office building. She hoped it wasn't nosy to ask, and was relieved when it didn't seem to offend her.

"I started out just renting an office for my business like most people do. But it became obvious quite quickly that I wouldn't get ahead financially by only operating a small bookkeeping firm. I looked at a lot of options before realizing that the best opportunity for me lay in the rent check I was writing to someone else every month.

I added as many clients as I could manage, moved back in with my parents to reduce my own expenses, and bought the first office building I could afford. Because I had my own small business, I knew what to do to make the building far more attractive to other people like me, and I've almost always had it fully occupied since I bought it eight years ago.

I poured every spare cent I had into paying off the mortgage early, and then I took a new mortgage out on it so I could purchase this building last year."

"Wait, so you own two office buildings?"

"That's correct." Janet was so matter-of-fact about her situation, Lisa almost couldn't believe it. If she owned anything, she'd be bragging to everyone about it!

"And you did it on your own. Wow!"

"Well, it wasn't without its sacrifices. I've worked hard and many people looked down on me for living with my parents at my age. But I can assure you, they don't look down on me anymore."

"I really could not live with my parents again, but I wish I could do what you did!"

"And why can't you?"

"I just… well… I don't know."

"Tell me Lisa, what do you really want?"

Lisa paused. She knew what she really wanted. It was something she had wanted since fifth grade. But it seemed so silly sometimes, even though she never stopped wanting it. At least Janet would tell her straight up if it was a bad idea…

"When I was in fifth grade, I had to write a report about the gold rush. Everyone else wrote about the miners who struck gold and got rich. But I thought the coolest story was about this lady. She went up to Alaska with her husband, and then he disappeared in the mountains and she was stuck with nothing except this little house and she only had enough money for one month's rent. So she moved her bed to the kitchen and rented out the rest of the house to miners who needed a place to sleep.

She made so much money that she moved to a bigger house and ran it as a proper boarding house. At the end of the gold rush, she had so much money she bought a hotel in San Francisco and ended up super rich. Since then I've always dreamed of running a sort of boarding house. Not like the place I live where a bunch of students trash the place, or an actual old-fashioned boarding house, but a place where professionals could stay that's really nice."

Janet smiled, "That's a brilliant idea! I would have much rather stayed with you than my parents, even if it cost more. And I know there are many people who would find it very convenient to live in a professionally run house like the one you've described."

"Really? Oh wow! I've never told anybody that because I thought they'd say it was stupid! My dad always told me my ideas were a waste of air."

"What you were told in the past makes no difference to your future unless you let it. It's up to you, Lisa. You can spend your days waitressing and cleaning, or you can build something bigger. I look forward to seeing you a week from Monday for your training week."

Janet gathered her briefcase and coat, so Lisa followed her in leaving.

"Janet?" Janet paused as she was about to lock her office door and looked straight at her.

"Thank you."

"You're welcome Lisa."

On the bus ride home, Lisa mulled over the conversation. There was a little spark of hope inside her that was a new sensation. It was one thing to hold onto a silly childhood dream. It was another thing to hear a professional adult tell her she had a good idea—and believe that she could make it happen!

This new feeling matched what Janet said about the past not mattering. Lisa was realizing that the things her dad had always said about her *were* lies. She *wasn't* lazy, or a waste of air, or any of the other things he said. It was time to quit thinking about the past and start thinking about the future.

The next day Lisa accepted an extra shift at the restaurant and used the chance to ask her boss if she could only work until three on weekdays. He didn't seem to care, and she was relieved she could work both jobs.

On her way back home, she stopped at an office supply store and bought a pad of grid paper and a packet of pencils. Sitting on her bed, she started to write down numbers.

$600 a week (taxes?) = $31,200 a year

$5,000 tuition for bookkeeping certificate = $25,000 starting salary

House price =?

Mortgage payments =?

Type of house =?

She had so many unanswered questions. It would be nice if she had parents who would give her advice, and maybe even help her out. All the other students living in the house talked about getting money from their parents as if it was a normal thing. Maybe that didn't really matter. Maybe she could do it herself and prove that a childhood dream could actually come true.

CHAPTER 10

On Monday after work Lisa went to the bank. She hoped the same account assistant would be there to help her but she didn't know her name. Fortunately, the name Kathleen Morgan was on the office door where they had met, so she made an appointment for the following day at 3:30.

The next day Lisa wanted to chicken out. How silly was it for a waitress to be asking about buying a house? But then she thought about Janet. *She* probably didn't care at all what people thought. So, she walked into the bank pretending to be confident and secure. Her confidence faltered after Ms. Morgan informed her that she was not a mortgage advisor, but Lisa explained that she wasn't ready to buy a house, she just wanted an idea of what she needed to do.

For some reason, this lady was willing to help her out, and Lisa was grateful. But the information seemed to put her dream out of reach.

"The bank generally looks at total household income. Since you are the household, you'll need an income of about $83,000, a down payment of $30,000, and excellent credit to qualify for a mortgage of $300,000." The one good thing was that Lisa was using her credit card and then paying the balance each month. That was only a small start to building good credit, but at least she was doing something right!

When she was back in her room, she wrote out the new numbers. It wasn't hopeless. If she actually made $31,000 as a janitor and could work up to making $44,000 as a bookkeeper, she would almost have the household income requirement. Then, she needed to save the down payment and get good credit.

Lisa had the beginning of a plan. She would try to make enough at the restaurant to cover her expenses and her college classes. Then everything she made as a janitor she could put into savings. In a few months, she'd go back to Janet and ask for her advice. Maybe if she was already saving and taking classes it would show Janet that she was serious about her plan.

The next day Lisa put into action the very smallest part of her plan. She changed her tips into bills at the end of her shift, and deposited all the bills at the bank machine on her way home. The tips had been fun spending money until now, but when she added up that cash, she realized it was a real opportunity. Even if she just made $20 in tips every day, that was an extra $400 every month!

In two weeks, she would have the payment for the Intro to Bookkeeping class that started in January. She was lucky to get into this class—the next one wasn't until March.

Lisa woke up excited, and a little nervous. Sure, she worked a lot of hours when she was still in high school but working two nearly full-time jobs at a time seemed more challenging. Although it wasn't like she had much else going on in her life. Most of the other students in the house were busy with school, and the only thing she'd miss out on was nighttime television.

By the time she was on the bus going to start her janitor training, she convinced herself that it was no big deal. She'd just do the job, work hard, and head home happy. Everything she did now was getting her a tiny bit closer to that big goal, so it was worth it. And now she had somewhere to wear the track suit that Chad had convinced her to buy in the summer. It had seemed silly to get exercise clothes when she never went to the gym, but he thought she needed clothes to 'hang out' in. Now at least she'd be able to move around easily while she cleaned!

Lisa thought she moved fast as a waitress, but Manuel had her beat. He also knew almost everyone who was still working in the offices when they got started by name, and Lisa despaired at ever remembering everyone. They all seemed friendly, but sad that this was Manuel's last week.

Although they worked hard and fast, all the instructions Manuel gave took time and it was still after ten when they finished for the day.

"Don't worry, Lisa. It will get easier over time. By the end of the week you'll already be starting to get your own system going."

Thanking him for all his guidance, she watched him lock up the office, waved goodbye to the security guard who covered the block of buildings, and then went to the bus stop to catch the bus home.

From this area the last bus ran at 11:30 pm, so she'd have to work hard to make sure she didn't miss it. She struggled to stay awake on the thirty minute ride home, and hoped she would quickly get used to this new, slightly crazy schedule.

Jennifer and Collette were at the table studying for an exam when she got in. It was nice to come 'home' to lights on and friendly faces. She loved having chats with the people in the house, instead of hiding from her dad and trying to ignore his complaining. It felt like a part of her was seeing the world in color for the first time, and she liked it.

Of course, she didn't tell anyone else about her past. It was obvious now that her parents were way different than other people's parents and she didn't like to bring attention to that fact. She brushed off questions by saying her parents were 'really busy' and it seemed to end further conversation.

After a quick shower she was relieved to climb into bed. She was used to her feet hurting after a shift at the restaurant, but tonight more than her feet hurt. And by the morning it was worse. She forced herself to keep up the pace while serving breakfast and lunch —but all she really wanted to do was get in a hot bath and soak her aching arms and back. It was small consolation to have another $30 in tips to put in the bank at the end of her shift.

The girls were back home after their exam. "Are you alright?" Jennifer asked, looking at her hobble into the kitchen.

"I am *so* sore! I swear, it's like I spend the whole night last night working out with some body building maniac! It was agony to try and get through my shift!"

"Definitely time for some ibuprofen!" Colette insisted before Lisa's cleaning shift with Manuel. It helped enough to get her through the rest of the night.

By Friday Lisa's body was already adjusting to the new demands she was placing on it. Although she was so tired when she got home at night that she fell asleep quickly, no matter how much her body hurt. She sometimes thought back to that first sleepless night at the house. It seemed like more than just a few months earlier. Now she had a plan for her life—a good one that she got excited about!

Saturday Lisa enjoyed the chance to sleep in. She got up late, ate one of the apples she kept in her room for breakfast, and gathered up her laundry. The house was supposed to have a washer and dryer, but the washer didn't drain completely leaving the clothes too wet to ever get dry in the old dryer. Plus, the washer smelled. It was easier to walk two blocks to the little laundromat and get everything done in an hour and a half.

Back home with all her laundry clean and dry, Lisa was bored. She didn't want to spend a lot of money on going out, so she ended up putting on a clean pair of jeans and a t-shirt and going back to the library for a few hours.

While she was on the bus, an ad on the window of an office supply store caught her eye. Something about laptops on sale for $800. Normally that would be way out of her budget. But with her new janitor job, she could maybe afford one.

The lack of a laptop was a concern when she attended the information night at the community college. While there was a computer room available for students, a counselor admitted that the computers were old and slow, and she'd be far better off with her own laptop. Her roommates all had their own computers and apparently the internet speed at the house was fast enough to keep up with whatever they needed. Lisa decided she'd ask Janet about buying a laptop if she got the chance.

When she got a call from the restaurant asking her to come in for a shift she jumped at the chance to do something—even work.

At the end of her shift she had made over $40 in tips, so when Chad asked if she wanted to see a movie and go out for a late dinner, she figured she deserved it. It was fun to hang out with him and have a few hours where she didn't have to be run off her feet.

CHAPTER 11

The first week in December was also Lisa's first full week of cleaning by herself. Night one started pretty good. She got the top floor done by six pm and was already looking forward to getting home by ten. But on the second floor, she didn't realize that one of the bags of garbage had a full cup of coffee in it that was leaking out. Her first clue that there was a problem was the lingering smell of coffee. When she turned around, there was a trail of coffee all the way across the carpet and along the tile floor.

It took Lisa half an hour to soak up all the liquid in the carpet, clean the stain, and wipe up the floor. She'd remember to be way more careful emptying the garbage cans, but for now it was all on her shoulders to get it cleaned up properly.

She felt tired and discouraged and it was hard to keep going. Finally, at 10:50 she was locking up and walking to the bus stop. As she walked, she had the creepy sensation of being followed. Not one to shy away, she stopped and turned around suddenly. It was just the security guard in his patrol car. He stopped to say hello and offered to stick around until the bus came. She left it up to him but was a little relieved when he pulled over into a parking lot and waited there until the bus came.

Friday afternoon Lisa put $125 in the bank from the week's tips, and when she arrived at the office building Janet gave her a deposit slip for the $1,100 that was already in her account. While Lisa knew she'd get paid every second Friday, actually having the money in her account was exciting! It made it feel like the hard work and late nights were worth it, and she powered through the cleaning, leaving by ten pm.

Saturday, after Lisa caught up on sleep and did her week's laundry, she took the bus to the office supply store she passed the week before. They were really pushing the laptop sales, and she spent quite a bit of time learning about the different options. Although it was tempting to just buy one, she didn't know if she needed anything specific for bookkeeping. So she took the saleslady's business card, promising to come back when she knew exactly what she needed to buy.

The next week Lisa caught Janet still in her office when she came by to do the cleaning. "Lisa! Come on in! How is everything going?"

"Hi Janet! It's going good thanks. I think I've got the hang of things here."

"Well the tenants I've spoken with are very pleased with the job you're doing!"

"Oh, good!" Lisa was trying to do more than Manuel taught her, taking time to do some extra cleaning on one floor each week. Of course, she started on the floor Janet's office was on, just in case she noticed.

"Hey, I was thinking of buying a laptop but I didn't know if I needed to look for anything special so I could use it to do bookkeeping stuff. Do you have any recommendations?"

Janet mentioned a few things to look for that Lisa hadn't considered. She also told her that she could probably find some freelance work

online after she finished her first year of classes. This was new information for Lisa, who thought only computer programmers worked
online. Janet also suggested she save so she could buy at least one of
the main accounting programs when she started her classes. It would
enable her to do far more than the basic free version allowed,
although that version would get her through the first lot of classes.

Armed with the new information, Lisa couldn't wait to get back to
the computer store on Saturday. It turned into a big day for her. Not
only did she buy her very first laptop, but she also went to the
community college, and paid the remaining $195 for the four week
Introduction to Bookkeeping course. It was a good thing she got into
the Saturday class. Although she was getting faster at cleaning,
losing hours for night school in the middle of her shifts would have
made it nearly impossible to finish in time to take the last bus home.

When she got back to the house, she got lots of attention from her
roommates for buying her own laptop. All of them were using
laptops their parents had given them, and it gave her a huge boost of
confidence to know that she could keep up with kids who were
funded by their parents. Everyone helped her get started, and by the
end of the night she was also slightly savvy in social media with her
first four online 'friends'. Nobody teased her about being so late to
the online trends. By now they all knew she was really on her own in
the world, and everything she did or got was through her own gutsy
approach to life.

Chad was trying to insist that she come home with him for Christmas, but she wasn't sure whether to accept. His parents sounded like
people with big expectations for their only child, and she didn't want
to get caught in the middle of some high-pressure family event for
the holidays. Part of her wished she could see her mom at Christmas,
but there was no way she was risking having her dad find out how
good she was doing, just in case he tried to take it away from her.

Manuel surprised her by checking in on Friday before she started
her cleaning shift. He brought his two sons who were fifteen and
seventeen years old. They often helped him do the cleaning during

holidays, and he wanted Lisa to meet them in case she ever needed to hire help. It hadn't occurred to Lisa that she *could* hire someone to help her out, but she took their information just in case. At least having a back-up plan was a good idea, and if they worked as hard as Manuel did, they'd be good to have around.

The following Friday, Janet met up with Lisa to give her the deposit slip for the two weeks. Again, she thanked Lisa for the good job she was doing and congratulated her on registering for her first course.

"I'm taking a week off over Christmas. Quite a few people will be gone over the holidays, so the cleaning should be easier. If you do run into any problems, call the security company and they'll take care of it. Oh, and remember, the entire building is closed Christmas Day and Boxing Day so you can enjoy a few days off in the middle of the week."

Lisa thanked her before going up to the third floor to start cleaning.

That weekend she transferred the numbers from her grid pad onto a spreadsheet on her laptop and updated them with her weekly earnings. She added another $190 in tips into savings and her first full two week payment for cleaning. In total her bank account had nearly $1,900 that she didn't need for living expenses.

Without family to buy Christmas presents for she wasn't doing much holiday shopping, although she wanted to get her roommates something as well as Janet and Manuel. She decided not to go to Chad's parents for Christmas once her boss at the restaurant offered her a shift on Christmas Day at double pay. The holidays had always been a disappointment, so she didn't have big expectations now that she was on her own.

CHAPTER 12

Three days before Christmas, Lisa arrived early to her cleaning shift with a Christmas flower arrangement to give Janet. She hadn't known what to get until she remembered how much her mom enjoyed receiving something similar from a family friend a few years ago. Lisa couldn't remember who that was, but her mom's happiness had left an impression.

Janet was working late trying to get things wrapped up before the holidays and was delighted with the gift. Lisa asked if she could have Manuel's address to bring him a gift too and was surprised that Janet knew it by memory. She told Lisa to call first to make sure he would be home, and also hinted that he loved a good whiskey, in case Lisa wasn't sure what to get him. Fortunately, Lisa hadn't bought him anything yet.

Saying goodbye to Janet, Lisa went to get started with the cleaning. Already people were taking off early for the holidays, and she was on the bus home just after nine. She got off one stop early so she could catch the liquor store before it closed. When she got home, she had to deal with some good-natured teasing, since everyone thought they should try what she bought before passing it on. It was nice to be home in time to hang out with her roommates before they left for the holidays. She'd be the only one there for the rest of the week, and it would feel lonely.

The next day Lisa was run off her feet at the restaurant. Apparently, everyone was eating out, and they were in a hurry to get their meals and leave again. Lisa didn't have the heart to leave the rest of the staff scrambling, and stayed until the early dinner rush was over. For the first time, she was late getting to the offices, arriving just as Janet was leaving at six pm.

"Lisa! I'm glad to see you. Is everything OK?"

"Hi Janet. Yep, I just stayed late at the restaurant because it was so busy. It seemed like everyone in the city wanted to eat out today!"

"Well, I can't blame them. Anyways, have a lovely Christmas."

Lisa returned the Christmas greetings and got to work cleaning. It looked like nobody had even been to work on the third floor, so after a quick check of the garbage and floors, and wiping down the bathrooms she was down to the second floor in record time. It was still 9:30 before she could lock up the whole building, but she hadn't rushed.

With a quick wave to the security guard, she boarded the bus for home. She was surprised at how reluctant she was to go home since everyone would be gone. For years she stayed in her room to avoid interactions with her dad, but now she loved living in a busy house where there was always someone to talk to. Even if they did eat any food she left in the kitchen, just as Chad predicted that first day they met!

When she walked in the front door, she was totally surprised to see that her roommates had set up a small (and quite tacky) Christmas tree on the kitchen table with a card and a gift bag beside it. Everyone had signed the card, and in the gift bag were three tiny bottles of whiskey with a note that said *Pace Yourself!* She found her eyes tearing up a bit at their thoughtfulness. She had bought them each their favorite candy or chocolate as a Christmas gift, but she really hadn't expected anything in return. And the Christmas tree was a nice touch, even with its gaudy ornaments!

Christmas Eve dawned bright and crisp. Lisa bundled up for the walk to the restaurant but ended up walking fast anyways, just to stay warm. She warned her boss that she needed to leave by four, but after rescuing him yesterday he was more than happy to let her go on time today. After quickly changing out of her waitressing clothes and grabbing Manuel's gift she boarded the first of the three buses she would need to take to get to his place.

Manuel lived in a gorgeous subdivision with big homes all covered in perfectly hung Christmas lights. Even before the sun went down, she could see how beautiful it would look at night. His oldest son Freddy answered the door and hollered for his dad. Manuel came to the door with his wife Betsy and introduced Lisa. She handed him his gift and thanked him for the great job he did training her.

Betsy was all smiles, "Come in, come in!"

"Oh, I can't, I've got to get to the office to start cleaning. But thank you! I hope you all have a really nice Christmas!"

"Are you going home for Christmas after work?" Manuel asked. She remembered telling him where she was from, but nothing about her family.

"No, I work at a restaurant too, and they've asked me to work tomorrow. I'll take Boxing Day off though, which will be nice."

"I see why you like her Manuel! Another hard worker like you!" Betsy smiled at her husband. "But Lisa, please come back on Boxing Day. You can borrow our family for the day!"

Lisa was so surprised at the invitation she couldn't think of a reason to say no. So she accepted and promised to be there early afternoon on the 26th. She walked back to the bus stop feeling a little awkward about the idea of spending a holiday with someone else's family. Oh well, it would be too rude to cancel, and it was just one day. She'd stay for a few hours and then slip out.

The office building was completely empty by the time she got there, and there wasn't much cleaning to do. On her way home a few short hours later Lisa was glad to have things to fill the next few days. Already she was looking forward to her roommates getting back!

Working Christmas Day was more fun than she expected. All the customers were grateful to everyone working, and there wasn't a single complaint about anything. The staff bonded over their 'working holiday' and pitched in to help each other out when it got busy. At the end of the day, Lisa made a record $75 in tips and had a happier Christmas than she would have at home with her parents. Now she just had to make it through a visit to Manuel's tomorrow and a few more days of quiet before everything picked up again.

When she walked up to Manuel's house the next day, she could tell there was something going on. She hoped that the jeans and white blouse she was wearing would be appropriate. The driveway and street were full of parked cars, and even outside she could hear the sounds of a party in full swing. She wasn't even sure anyone would hear the doorbell, but Betsy must have been right there waiting.

"Lisa! It's so wonderful to see you! Come in! Come in!" She wrapped an arm around Lisa and brought her into the house. "Everybody this is Lisa who took over Manuel's job at the office!"

A chorus of hellos greeted her, and after taking her coat Betsy walked her to the kitchen, introducing her as she went. From what Lisa could figure out, they had a really big extended family, and everyone was over at the same time. When they got to the kitchen Lisa found herself with a glass of sparkling wine in her hand and an aunt of Betsy's asking her all about herself. Normally reserved around new people, Lisa found herself chatting and enjoying herself far more than she expected. It was such a warm and happy family that she couldn't help but feel welcomed.

Two hours of visiting later, she made her way to the rec room where Freddy and his younger brother Marco, along with a half dozen other teens, convinced her to take a turn at playing *Just Dance* on the Wii. They all agreed she needed a lot of practice, but she *did* keep up with them for quite a while. Lisa was secretly pleased that she was in such good shape, and once she was out of the final round, she had a great time laughing with everyone else who was watching.

When it was time to eat, the aunts and Betsy rounded up everyone in the dining room for grace, before they started digging into the huge buffet laid out on the family-sized table. One of the aunts made sure to point out the *Pepian*, "This is the best dish for the holidays!"

"What's in it?" Although she was familiar with Mexican food, these dishes seemed a little different, and the aromas wafting from the table were making her mouth water.

"It's chicken, with our secret family sauce, roasted sesame seeds, tomatoes, and lots of spices. Delicious!"

Another aunt took Lisa under her wing, and 'helped' add food to her plate until she laughingly insisted she'd drop it if anything more was put on. She followed the other adults into the living room and found a seat off to the corner while she tried to make a dent in all the delicious food.

After a while, Manuel found her and made himself comfortable in a vacant chair beside her. "So Lisa, how are you finding your new family?"

Lisa looked at him, confused. "I'm not sure what you mean?"

"Anyone who buys me whiskey is officially family! So you're stuck with us now!"

"Oh!" She smiled, "I've never been with such a happy group of people before. You guys are really great! Does everyone live nearby?"

"Just about. We've worked really hard to have everyone here. It's taken a while. My dad was the first one to move here from Central America in the 1980s. He started one of the first ethnic food trucks in the city, and as his business grew more of us could come over. Now we're three generations living in the city, with five different family businesses, two nurses, and three teachers. This country has been good to us!"

"Sounds like you all are pretty hard workers! When did you start the office cleaning?"

"Oh, that was just something extra I picked up a few years ago. I had sold my home maintenance business and was going to retire, but Betsy was still working nightshift as a nurse and I got bored. You know, retiring seems like a good idea until you actually try it. Boring!

Janet does the bookkeeping for all our family businesses and when I told her I needed something to do she offered me the janitor position. So I did the cleaning until Betsy retired too! Now we're just a couple of old people ready for retirement. When the boys have both graduated, we'll take a motorhome and explore the country for a year."

Lisa found out much later that Manuel and Betsy adopted Freddy and Marco when their parents had both been killed. They were related in some distant way, and when the childless couple heard about the two orphans they immediately put their lives on hold to go and rescue them. It made her even more proud to be friends with such kind and giving people.

"Wow! That's really cool! I've never been anywhere except here and my hometown." They were interrupted by some other men demanding that Manuel come join them in a ping pong tournament. He tried to convince Lisa to come too, but she refused. Dancing was enough 'sport' for her for one day!

She took her empty plate to the kitchen and found herself with a tea towel drying dishes. There seemed to be a real split between the men and the women, with the women taking care of most of the food and kitchen duties. But what she didn't see was any attitude from the men. Everyone seemed genuinely kind and loving, and the women in the kitchen were continuously interrupted by their men coming in to thank them for all the good food and offering to help clean up.

When the men finally all cleared out of the kitchen, Betsy gave Lisa a wink. "Manuel may know how to clean a whole office building, but I refuse to let him try to clean my kitchen."

Lisa was surprised at how long she stayed. When she finally pulled out her phone to look at the time, she realized she needed to get going or she might miss catching the last bus. She thanked Betsy for the invitation and the best Boxing Day she ever had. Betsy gave her a big hug. "If you need anything, you just call us OK? We have lots of time now, and we're happy to help you out if you need." Lisa soaked up the good feelings from the hug and all the kind words she had heard over the day. It was nice to know there were such happy families in the world.

CHAPTER 13

The days after Christmas were surprisingly busy at the restaurant. It was a welcome distraction while Lisa waited for the time to pass for her roommates to come home, and her first class to start. On the first Friday in January everyone was back, and she had another deposit from Janet in the bank. With tips, her account was now up to $3,250, but she knew some of that would have to go to paying taxes as Janet had mentioned. She was hoping for a chance to talk to her again soon about anything else she should be saving money for, but by the time she got to the offices, Janet had already left for the weekend.

The next day Lisa was up early and excited about starting her first class. She had never enjoyed high school (except for Accounting class with Mr. Shoud). It was just a safe place to stay away from her dad. Now she was actually going to learn about things that could help her have a career and do something she liked doing. It was a nice change!

The other students in the class were a mix of ages and backgrounds. Lisa was the youngest at eighteen and the oldest was a lady in her fifties, who wanted to switch careers and start bookkeeping.

Everyone seemed nice, and happy to spend their Saturday in the classroom. Lisa forgot to buy something ahead of time for lunch so she followed nearly everyone else to the café in the building. She decided she wouldn't feel guilty about spending a bit more on buying lunch out. With the extra tips that came in over Christmas, she could spend some cash without a problem. And it was interesting to sit back and listen to the conversations as everyone started to get to know each other.

With two jobs and Saturday classes, Sundays were now Lisa's only day off. She slept in, got her laundry done, and then spent the rest of the day doing as little as possible. Having her own computer meant she could check out property sites, and slowly learn more about mortgages and buying a house, but she did this while laying on her bed and only got up when Chad knocked on her door to offer some leftover pizza.

By the second Saturday Lisa was certain she wanted to follow through and get her Professional Bookkeeping Certificate. Everything in bookkeeping had a rule, and good bookkeeping required that the rules be followed. It felt like she had found a career that made her feel secure, although it seemed weird to think about it that way.

She knew she could earn the $5,000 needed for classes and supplies with her janitor job and tips. And the first seven courses were available on Saturdays, so she could take them while working both jobs. As long as she passed each course, she could take them one after the other.

The bigger problem might come further down the line, where the courses were only available in the evenings or online. With her challenges reading, she felt more comfortable learning in a classroom setting. But that was still eight or nine months away. Most of the classes right now were one month of all day Saturdays. She needed to keep working hard in class while earning as much money as possible.

When she saw Janet next, she asked her about taxes. Janet

suggested they set aside an hour to go over everything. They agreed to meet on Sunday afternoon at a coffee shop near Lisa's house.

Friday night Lisa was excited to finish her work week and get to her next class on Saturday. She wasn't prepared for the aftermath of a flu bug that had hit the top floor offices. It took her more than an hour to get the bathrooms cleaned because she kept on having to leave the bathrooms to get a break from the smell. The bathrooms were supposed to have air fresheners, but they weren't helping. She had to run to catch the last bus and sank into the seat relieved that the evening was over.

On Sunday she struggled to get up and get going. She wanted to get her laundry done before meeting Janet for coffee, but she was so tired. There was just enough time to toss the bag of clean laundry on her bed before heading out to meet Janet.

"Are you OK Lisa? You look pale."

"I think I just need a good night's sleep tonight! I can't believe how tired I've been this weekend. But I'm OK thanks."

Janet reviewed Lisa's financial situation with her and seemed pleased with the amount Lisa had saved already. She didn't expect that Lisa would have to pay additional taxes on her earnings in December, since she hadn't been working full-time until July and the restaurant was probably deducting more tax than needed. For the new year, Lisa could claim her college tuition against her taxable earnings, but Janet advised her to set aside 15% of everything she made cleaning to prepare for the extra she would still have to pay.

Since Lisa didn't have a complicated tax return, Janet offered to help her file it as soon as she got her tax summary from the restaurant in February. That was way ahead of the April deadline, but Janet wouldn't have spare time to work with her after February because that was her busiest time. Lisa was already keeping all her receipts and records, even though there wasn't much yet. She could use her insurance fees as a business expense but without having to buy supplies she didn't have any other tax write offs.

They finished a little earlier than an hour, and Lisa went home and went straight to bed. All she could think about was getting some sleep. But in the middle of the night, she woke up and ran to the bathroom where she was violently ill. She hoped she didn't wake up any of her roommates, but she didn't have the energy to make it back to her bedroom. Laying down beside the toilet she curled up in a ball and tried not to moan.

"Lisa? Are you OK? Oh my gosh, did you actually get wasted?" Lisa opened one eye to see Chad leaning over her. Sun was shining through the small bathroom window. Every inch of her body hurt, and she was freezing cold.

"No, sick."

"Oh, man. Well, I need to use the bathroom. Can you move?" She managed to get up and drag herself to her room. She called her manager and told him she couldn't work. As soon as the rest of the house left for school, she crawled back to the bathroom, so she had less distance to travel when she needed it.

In between dozing off, she tried to figure out what to do about cleaning the office. Remembering Manuel had offered his sons to help out she gave him a call. He was more than happy to help out. Freddy had basketball practice, but Manuel and Marco could do the cleaning for her tonight. He asked for her address so he could come to collect the keys and then Lisa quickly cut him off to be sick again.

She couldn't remember the last time she had been sick. It was beyond awful, and all she wanted was someone to take care of her and make this horrible feeling go away. When the doorbell rang a few hours later she dragged herself to the front door. Betsy and Manuel were both there.

"Oh, my poor girl! Here, let's get you back to bed. I brought some stuff." Betsy wrapped her arm around Lisa and followed Lisa's lead back to her bedroom. In no time she tucked Lisa into a re-made bed, set up the basket/bedside table with crackers, ginger ale, and a pretty box of Kleenexes, and had neatly folded her bag of clean laundry and put it away. Overwhelmed with her kindness, Lisa found tears streaming down her cheeks.

"Thank you, Betsy. I'm sorry I'm such a mess."

"Don't you worry about it! I brought some soup that I'll put in the fridge. You might not feel up to eating today, but try to eat something tomorrow OK? Now, where are the office keys?"

Lisa directed her to her purse where she kept the keys. Manuel popped his head in her bedroom door long enough to tell her he'd cover the cleaning until she felt better. When they left, Lisa fell asleep and slept straight through until the evening. She woke up feeling shaky and exhausted but was able to clean herself up a bit in the bathroom before going back to bed. Just before she fell asleep again, she texted the restaurant to say she wouldn't be in for the rest of the week. She knew it was bad manners to text in sick, but she had no energy to talk.

By Thursday Lisa was recovering. Her roommates had been very understanding, offering to get her things, and leaving silly 'Get Well' cards in the bathroom. They even left Betsy's soup for her, which she was finally able to slowly eat. She called Manuel on Friday and asked if he could do one more night of cleaning for her. He was happy to hear she was feeling better and offered to bring back the keys on Sunday if she thought she was up to going back to work the next day. Thanking him and Betsy for all their kindness and help, she hung up and went back to bed.

When she woke up again, she felt like she was thinking clearly for the first time all week. Calling Janet, she left a message asking her to call back. She had a feeling Manuel would try to not get paid for the week, but Lisa didn't want to take advantage of his kindness. Janet would tell her how to handle it.

The restaurant had left a few messages that Lisa ignored. But now she felt like she could handle talking to her manager. After hearing how sick she had been, he suggested she wait until the next Wednesday to start working again as long as her symptoms didn't come back. Right after, Janet called. She reassured Lisa that she had done everything right in getting Manuel to cover her shifts. Yes, Lisa should pay Manuel for the week of cleaning. For this time, it would be OK to write him a check from her personal account.

Saturday Lisa felt like a bear stepping out of its cave after hibernating. At least she felt well enough to go to her class. But she still had some recovering to do, and by eight pm she was fast asleep. Sunday she slept more, picked up a Thank You card to give Manuel with a check inside when he dropped off the keys, and did her laundry. Her clothes were all looser on her than they were at the beginning of the week and she hoped she would go back to her usual size soon.

The week off hurt her finances. With no tips or hours from the restaurant, she needed to use some of her savings. Although she was relieved to still be able cover her expenses, it was frustrating to feel like she was further away from her goal.

But when she reviewed her numbers at the end of January, she realized she was still making progress, just a little slower than planned. Her savings account was at $3,335 after paying for her first course in the bookkeeping program.

For the next four months, she could take one course each month. Classes were every Saturday from nine to four. Her biggest challenge would be finding time to study in between both jobs. She knew from experience that she needed more time than other people to practice what she was learning in order for it to stick. But since this was all information she would be using in real life as a bookkeeper she was motivated to learn it.

CHAPTER 14

February was cold, wet, and gray. Lisa settled into her new, busier routine and tried not to think about the miserable weather. Colette's mom was a flight attendant, and found Colette and Jennifer cheap flights to Mexico for their February break. Everyone in the house wished they were going along. Mark was going skiing in the Rockies with his family. Chad was sticking around for the week, but Lisa didn't have any time to hang out with him. When she wasn't working, she was either studying or sleeping.

While the restaurant was much slower in February Lisa still had the same hours to work, just with lower tips. Her average was down to $50 a week, and some days it was just pocket change at the end of a shift. She still tried to put as much of it into savings as possible, and along with her janitor pay she increased her savings to $5,200 after paying for her next course in March.

On Janet's advice, she opened a separate business account for her janitor income, where she kept aside the 15% extra she would likely need to pay taxes. Janet cautioned her to be prepared for a much higher tax rate when she no longer had tuition to claim and was making a higher income as a bookkeeper. To get into the bank to open a new account she cut her restaurant shift short and then got to the office building late after the appointment. It was a good thing she didn't need to fit in many appointments since traditional office hours were spent working or taking the bus to work.

Lisa also spent an hour and a half in Janet's office at the end of February to file her taxes. Last year her high school accounting teacher Mr. Shoud helped her file her taxes. As a student working a part-time job at the café, she received a tax refund for all the income tax she paid for the year. When Janet recorded all the income for this tax return, it was still quite close to the minimum threshold. But the $234 she was getting as a refund would be her last one.

With almost full-time hours at the restaurant and the full-time cleaning job, Lisa was definitely in the taxpaying category now. Her tuition costs would help keep her tax bill lower, but she felt good about making enough money to pay taxes. Somehow it seemed like a grown-up thing to do.

Lisa spent her breaks at the restaurant and her bus rides trying to study. She thought she'd be able to study on Sundays, but after six days in a row of going nonstop she needed a break. Chad was always trying to convince her to go out when she wasn't working. He was in his third year of business management and seemed to get A's without even trying. The one Saturday night they went out for a late dinner Lisa fell asleep at the table! They compromised by going to a movie on Sunday afternoons after she finished her laundry. Even then she sometimes found herself dozing off in the dark theater.

Betsy kept in touch with Lisa, checking in by text once or twice a week. She even came by the office building one night with hot chocolates for them and sat with her for a short break and visit. Lisa slowly told her about her childhood and why she didn't have any contact with her parents. It was only with Betsy's encouragement that Lisa called her mom at the beginning of March to wish her a Happy Birthday.

That phone call left Lisa feeling confused. It was nice to hear her mom's voice and know that she was doing OK. But she still felt angry that her mom was so controlled by her dad. Even though he wasn't around when Lisa called in the evening, she felt like her mom was talking as if he was listening in. Her own birthday two weeks later passed by quietly. Chad was the only one who knew when it was, and he was down with the flu. Lisa gave him a wide berth at the house, conscious of how much it cost her to be sick.

At the end of March her savings had jumped to $5,260 and Lisa took a moment to sit back and smile. Sure, at this rate she'd be working two jobs for a while and getting her salary high enough to qualify for a mortgage would still be hard, but she was on her way to buying her own house one day, probably before she was twenty-five.

In April Lisa enjoyed her first three-check month from her cleaning job. While the restaurant paid on the 1st and 15th of every month, as a janitor she received a deposit every other Friday. April she was a month where she got three deposits, so her savings got another boost to $8,300.

Although she wasn't the top student in her classes — and never would be — she was doing well and understanding everything. Learning things that she knew she'd use made it easier to study. She was also getting to know a few of the students who were following the same track as her. In May her teacher would be the same one she had in February and looking forward she would probably see more of the same teachers. That helped too because she already knew what to expect from each one.

After she finished her May class, she had the chance to switch to an online option for her next class. Most of the other students were taking this route because they could get a two-month course done in a matter of weeks. Lisa really wanted to speed up her schooling so she could get a bookkeeping job as soon as possible, but she didn't think she'd be able to learn the information without going to class. Finally, she decided it would be best if she kept to the classroom. She didn't want to risk failing a course even if it took longer to finish.

By June Lisa cracked the $10,000 mark in her bank account. She could hardly believe it. Writing numbers and goals down on paper was one thing. Actually seeing her account balance was another. But her years of keeping her savings a secret from her parents made her cautious about telling anyone her big news. Everyone around her knew she worked hard and was careful with her spending, but she was pretty sure no one would believe her anyways if she told them what she had saved already. That was OK. Knowing she was closer every month to buying a house made it all worth it.

With all the university students except Chad back home for the summer, the house was suddenly very quiet. Sometimes Chad would invite friends over to hang out at night, but often he was out later than Lisa. A big part of her really missed the freedom to go out whenever, have fun, and spend money without regrets. After last summer, she knew the fun she was missing out on.

Even though she could get away with paying for a night out with friends, she couldn't miss the study time. The current course was more challenging than the first five and Lisa struggled to keep up. She often stayed later on Saturdays to talk to the teacher, and make sure she knew the homework before leaving. The first week she completely failed the assignment, and she was terrified she might not make it through. At least the teacher was patient with her and gave her a chance to resubmit the assignment. As it was, she often emailed her teacher during the week when she got stuck.

When she successfully completed the course Lisa's confidence grew significantly. It was the most difficult academic thing she had ever done, but on her final assignment and test she got A's. While she felt the teacher deserved a lot of credit for the extra time and attention he had given her, he assured her that she had proven she knew the material well.

She was almost halfway through the program, her savings account was at $14,100, and she was used to her schedule now. Her body had adjusted to the demands of being on her feet all day, and cleaning into the night and she didn't have to fight to stay awake on the bus rides home.

In August she finally caught Janet with some time to chat. After a very busy tax season, Janet had taken time off to help care for her dad who had a stroke. The first thing Lisa noticed was that Janet looked tired for the first time since she had known her. Even though there was a care aide to help with his personal care, Janet admitted that the new responsibility was a challenge.

"But enough about my troubles Lisa. I want to know how you're doing."

Lisa shared about her school success and her growing savings account. It made her feel fantastic to hear how impressed Janet was with her progress. It was nice to have someone she could talk to about her goals. Janet challenged her to think about saving more than a 10% down payment for her first mortgage, which could save on interest. Lisa didn't really want to think about waiting longer to buy her first house, but she respected Janet and decided to talk to the lady at the bank about it when she got a chance. Plus, she'd need to get a better paying job than waitressing after she got her book-keeping certificate or her chances of getting a good mortgage were slim.

"Is there anything else besides school that I should do so I can get a good job when I'm done?"

Janet paused for a moment and then took a photograph out of her desk drawer. Handing it to Lisa, she sat back and waited for Lisa to look at it. The picture was of a girl with long dyed black hair and heavy eye makeup, wearing a black turtleneck, black ripped jeans, and black Doc Martens. She looked vaguely familiar.

"Is this your daughter?"

"No, that's me over twenty years ago."

"No way! Janet! I would never have guessed. Holy cow! What happened?"

"After I finished bookkeeping school with the top marks in the class, I was certain I could just walk into any company and they'd fall over themselves to offer me a job. But no one even gave me a follow-up call once they met me face-to-face. I failed every single interview. I had no idea why they wouldn't hire me. After my ninth interview with no results I got frustrated, and called up the HR lady to ask why they didn't hire me. She said that my look got in the way of my abilities, and they'd rather have a less qualified bookkeeper who looked like she could be trusted to manage their finances."

"Ouch. People really think that?"

"At first I didn't believe her. I went back and called every person who had interviewed me. They either gave me some story about finding someone more suitable, or they told me flat out that my image got in the way of my qualifications. After I got over my hurt feelings, I realized I needed some help if I was ever going to land a job. I hired a stylist who helped me create a professional image. Then I reapplied at three of the places that already turned me down, using my middle name and a new resume. Even though they realized who I was as we started the new interviews, they were all eager to hire me with my 'new look'. I took the highest offer from the three and never looked back."

"They ALL offered you a job?"

"Every single one. I still wish that organizations would hire people just on their qualifications, but until that happens image matters. I don't think you'd create the same problems with your current look but creating a polished image will pay for itself over and over. When I started my own business, I had no trouble attracting clients. That's credit to my skills *and* the way people perceive me."

Janet paused to shift to her computer. "I've sent you the contact information for the stylist I used. Try not to be offended by her first appraisal of you. It's probably the harshest anyone will speak to you, but once it's out of the way she'll make you look and feel the part of a business professional."

Lisa didn't think anyone could top her dad for insults and cruel remarks, but she kept that to herself. Thanking Janet for her help and time, she got up to start her cleaning shift. The routine was such a part of her nights now that she could work straight through without much thought. That gave her time to dream about her future when she'd have her boarding house set up, and she'd be in charge of her own little world.

CHAPTER 15

During her next break at the restaurant, Lisa called the stylist Janet had recommended. She left a quick voicemail and turned back to her studying for the rest of her break. The new course was Level 2 Financial Accounting, and she loved it. The hard work she put in the months before was paying off, and she was finding it much easier to grasp the concepts that were behind the accounting procedures.

On the bus to the office later, the stylist called her back. She offered Lisa a one-hour trial interview in September to see if she was a good candidate for her services. By the time Lisa hung up she felt like *she* was the one on trial, not the stylist. And at $50 for the hour, it wouldn't be cheap, either. But she was still amazed at the two different images of Janet, and she wanted to see if she could have the same transformation.

Three weeks later, Lisa was sitting in a small chair at a round table in an office downtown. The walls were covered in Before and After pictures that were truly impressive. She was already sold on the whole plan before McKenzie Stewart walked in. With deep red wavy hair, perfect makeup, and a forest green off the shoulder knitted sweater over white jeans and gold heels, McKenzie was a walking advertisement for her services. Lisa stood up to shake her hand and was surprised that they were the same height. McKenzie gave off an impression that she was tall and powerful. In comparison, Lisa felt rather dumpy and plain.

McKenzie made it very clear that she only worked with people who were committed to maintaining their new look. *If* she took on Lisa, she would have to sign a contract agreeing to follow McKenzie's advice for the next twenty-four months or face a fine. Although Lisa thought it was a bit excessive, she had to admit the pictures on the wall gave her confidence.

The next task would take a day off work for hair and makeup (*who needed a day to do that?* Lisa wondered) and another day off work for clothes shopping. The fee was $800, plus a minimum $1200 for clothes. Lisa just about snorted out loud until she realized McKenzie was completely serious. That was a full month set back in her savings plan! No matter how much she wanted to look professional and feel confident, she didn't think she could spend $2000 on it.

She thanked McKenzie for her time, paid the consultation fee, and found the bus that would take her to the offices so she could start cleaning. Although she knew a better image was important, she struggled with the idea of paying so much for it.

When she got home, Jennifer and Colette were sitting at the table eating ice cream sundaes. They invited Lisa to join them and she happily agreed. As they ate, she told them about her consultation with McKenzie. While Jennifer thought of it as an investment that would pay off—especially if it was the difference between getting a job and not getting a job—Colette wasn't so sure.

"Just go to a salon and get hair and make-up coaching from them. You're not exactly a mess Lisa, you just need to freshen your look and add a bit of style. I'll bet there's stores that offer personal shopping services that will cost less than what that lady will charge."

Lisa laughed, "This is a way harder decision than becoming a bookkeeper! I guess I'll just run it around in my mind until I know what I want. Thanks for the advice!"

Together they cleaned up the ice cream, syrups, sprinkles, and whipped cream and then Lisa said goodnight and went to bed feeling good. Having people to talk to was one of the benefits of living in a house like this. It was nice!

At the restaurant the next day she really paid attention to the people she was serving. It was true, she could see how some looked professional and others looked too casual, especially when Lisa knew they were coworkers. Later, when she stopped at the bank to deposit her week's tips, she realized that Kathleen Morgan (the lady who helped her get her first credit card and talked to her about mortgages) was one of those who always looked professional.

She finished her deposit, and then knocked on her open office door.

"Lisa! How nice to see you! Come in!"

"Oh, thanks Ms. Morgan. I can't believe you remembered my name." Lisa sat down in the chair across the desk from the account assistant.

"When I was much younger, I took a one-day seminar on improving your memory. It was an excellent investment and helps me with things like remembering client names. What can I do for you?"

"Well, I'm about halfway through my bookkeeping course, so next year I'll be ready to start applying for jobs. But I don't know how to look professional. I went to one lady who could help, but it would cost at least $2,000 and I wasn't sure if I should spend that kind of money. I noticed you always look professional. What do you think I should do?"

"Thank you for noticing! It's a bit of work to keep up this look so it's nice when it's appreciated. Personally, I wouldn't spend that much on a new image. But I do think you could update your look, and start building a work wardrobe. I can certainly recommend a great hair stylist. Sheila has been doing my hair and both of my daughter's hair for years, and she's fantastic. And if you go see her, she can probably recommend other people who can help you out. Plus, she's very reasonably priced, especially compared to some of the downtown salons."

Armed with the recommendation, Lisa thanked Ms. Morgan for her help, and headed to the offices. She felt better about doing a little bit at a time to be ready for job interviews, and grateful that Janet had brought the whole thing up and started Lisa thinking about next steps.

She wondered if she'd be able to keep her janitor job when she started working as a bookkeeper. If she couldn't, she'd need to find another way to earn more money than just her salary. Maybe she could switch to waitressing on the weekends if her weekdays were full. But in the meantime, she had two steady jobs that were helping her move up the savings ladder. Her account had just crossed the $16,000 mark.

On the last Sunday in September, Lisa got up earlier than usual so she could get her laundry done before going to Sheila's salon. When Lisa told her that she needed a more professional look, Sheila immediately got all the ladies there involved in handing out advice. Some things just made them laugh. A tiny elderly lady getting a perm told Lisa to "keep the girls up and obvious and make sure the boss sees 'em"!

One lady gave Lisa the name of a salesperson who worked at a department store makeup counter and could show her some tips for free. Another talked about getting her eyebrows done regularly (something Lisa had never even thought of), and always wearing smart, clean dress shoes.

The conversation morphed into the worst things they had ever seen in an office. While Lisa would never wear sweatpants to work, or a see-through top, she thought a nice pair of jeans would be OK. She was glad to know not to do that!

When Sheila finished styling Lisa's hair, they all ooohed and aaahed over her new look. Lisa had always worn her hair long and back in a braid or ponytail. Now, she had soft side bangs that somehow made her eyes and cheekbones more obvious, and her hair was just past her shoulders with long layers. She could still put it up in a braid or ponytail but wearing it down was now a nice option. Sheila suggested she come back in six weeks for a trim. With McKenzie's statement about keeping up your look still in the back of her mind, Lisa booked the appointment. She could start by keeping her hair looking good and add more changes to her look as she felt comfortable.

Lisa's roommates were so impressed with her new hairstyle they insisted on all heading down the street to the bar for a drink to celebrate. She thought she'd feel uncomfortable with all the attention on her, but she enjoyed it. At least while it was with people she knew. When Jennifer started trying to get other guys to talk to Lisa, she claimed she needed to go home and get some studying done before it was too late.

Chad left with her, and as they walked home he asked if she was ever planning on dating. Most girls he knew would love attention from other guys, but Lisa seemed different.

"I know there's lots of people in good relationships, but I spent the first eighteen years of my life watching my dad beat down my mom and I with his words. I just figured relationships aren't worth it if that's what can happen. I like being able to do my own thing and being in charge of my own life."

Chad claimed there were guys who would let a girl do that, but Lisa wasn't about to go trying to find out. She loved the feeling she got every time she finished a class, or saw her savings go up, and she wasn't about to trade that all in just so she could say she had a boyfriend.

CHAPTER 16

By the time December came, Lisa had a new dilemma. The next course was only available on Tuesday and Thursday evenings unless she took it online. Each class was three hours long, and the college was a twenty minute walk from the offices Lisa cleaned. There was no way she could work her cleaning around the classes. Without a solution, she postponed her registration until the next start date in February. At least she had some free time in December now to pick up as many shifts at the restaurant as possible. She knew it would be good tips for the whole time.

She'd spend Christmas Day at the restaurant working, and Manuel and Betsy already made sure that Lisa would join them on Boxing Day for their annual get-together. Now that she knew them better, and knew how much fun their family was, she was looking forward to it. They invited her to different events throughout the year, but Lisa was always busy working or studying. It was one of the small sacrifices she had made to chase her dream.

It wasn't until the evening on Boxing Day that Manuel settled beside her in the living room. "So Lisa, how are things working out for you?"

Lisa admitted she had done really well at her classes, but now she wasn't sure how to continue. She wanted to keep the janitor job but couldn't fit it in with the new class times in February. Manuel asked if she had considered hiring someone to cover Tuesdays and Thursdays for her at the offices.

"Can I do that? The only time I had someone work for me was when you covered when I was sick!"

"Sure you can. Pay someone a little less than what you get paid, and you can keep earning money on the days you're in school. You're still the one responsible for getting the job done, but if you can find someone reliable then it's the perfect solution. And I have someone in mind, if you're interested."

"Oh, I couldn't have you working for less than you made before!"

"Not me, Marco! He's sixteen now, and he's had a hard time finding a job he can just do in the evenings. All of his sports are after school so that rules out a lot of jobs. Plus, I trained him to help me out when I was still working, so it wouldn't take long to get him up to speed."

"Manuel, that's fantastic! I'd love to hire Marco. Let me see, I get $120 per night, so what if I pay him $100 per night? Or should it be more?"

"If you pay him that much, he'll have crazy ideas about how much he can make. How about $10 an hour, so $60 per night? That's still a good amount for a sixteen year old, and I can be available in case he gets stuck."

"Thank you! Wow, you and Betsy are just the gift that keeps on giving! Can I ask him now if he wants the job?"

Marco was ecstatic about the job offer. It was nice to be around a teen who was so keen to work. Lisa had to run the plan past Janet to get a second set of keys, but Manuel assured her it wouldn't be a problem.

The next day Lisa got to the offices a little early and stopped to check in with Janet. As Manuel predicted, Janet was fine with Lisa bringing in Marco as a sub-contractor. She had an extra set of keys that she gave Lisa right away and reminded Lisa to pay him out of her business account so she could keep track of her expenses.

Cleaning was much easier with so many people away on holidays, and Lisa was on her way home early with a sigh of relief. Between the restaurant and cleaning, she'd be working almost non-stop for the next few days, but she wanted to make the most of the big tips that would keep coming in until January hit and everyone cut back on their spending.

Lisa decided she'd start the New Year as she planned to go on — working, making money, and moving towards her dreams. On the 31st, the restaurant didn't say goodbye to the last customer of the year until almost ten pm, and she went home and slept until noon the next day. Without any classes this month she felt a little lost when she woke up. While it would be nice to have Saturdays free, she found she really loved everything she was learning. For someone who struggled through high school, the success she was enjoying on her course made her feel invincible.

She was doing great in both her jobs, learning skills in college that she would use in a new career, and saving more each month than she had dreamed possible. On January 1st she took a few minutes to look over her earnings for the year and she was pleased to see it was above $40,000. The extra hours she always took advantage of at the restaurant really helped top up her set income cleaning.

The rest of the students in the house were working hard on their theses, dissertations, or final exams. While they were all excited to finish school and move on, there was also a sense of sadness about leaving the house. They assured Lisa that she had lucked out by getting a group of roommates who all got along and treated the house with some measure of respect. As the only one planning on staying, Lisa would face a whole new set of roommates. She hoped it would be tolerable.

CHAPTER 17

At the end of April Lisa's savings were up to $30,500 but her spirits were low as she said goodbye to the people who had been her first real friends. They all promised to keep in touch, but it wouldn't the same as sharing a house together. Lisa had always thought of herself as a loner, but when the first of May hit and she really was alone in the house, she was devastated. She wondered if she'd be able to recreate the feeling from the full house when she had her own boarding house up and running. It was like they had become a family of sorts, and Lisa loved coming home every night to a place where she felt she belonged.

With the end of her classes in sight, and needing to keep busy and distracted while missing her roommates, Lisa threw herself into improving her image whenever she wasn't working or studying. She went to the make-up counter at the department store that the lady at Sheila's salon had recommended and came out looking like an older version of herself. It was weird to see herself in the mirror, and for the first few days she took forever to remember what went on in what order when she put on her makeup in the morning.

Perhaps the best indication of the impact of her new look was the increase in tips. She wanted to tell her customers off for being so shallow, but she kept her mouth shut and added the extra tips to her savings.

Building up a work wardrobe was more of a challenge until Lisa saw a magazine cover at the grocery store check-out with a 'Capsule Wardrobe for Businesswomen' headline. The whole article talked about which key wardrobe pieces to buy to have a lot of variety without spending a lot of money. Lisa loved the idea of having more work outfits for less money! She took the entire magazine with her shopping, and the salespeople she showed it to helped her buy very similar pieces to the pictures in the article. Having everything work together so well would make choosing an outfit every morning a lot easier.

She surprised herself by feeling drawn to colorful pieces when she started shopping. Although her base color was gray, and she picked up dress trousers, skirts, and a dress in different gray shades, all the tops she chose were bright and colorful. With her dark eyes and dark hair, she was suddenly seeing a new, professional, put-together version of herself that she hadn't even known existed. The final pieces to go with her wardrobe included a pair of short gray dress boots, and tall black boots that she could wear with her skirts and dress. She felt ready for the next phase in her life—one as a working professional woman.

Since there were students finishing courses every month at the college, there was no ceremony to mark the end of the program for Lisa. She just stopped by reception at the beginning of June and picked up her certificate. She completed all her courses with A's and B's and felt immensely proud of her accomplishment.

Desperate to do something to celebrate and wanting to erase the painful memories of her high school graduation from her mind, Lisa asked Janet, Manuel, and Betsy if she could take them out for dinner to celebrate. Aware that any one of them might try to pay on the sly, she made reservations at one of the city's top-rated restaurants in person and made sure her credit card would be used to pay for the meal.

While she was downtown, she splurged on a real grown-up going out outfit. Without a mom or best friend to rely on for advice she had to count on the saleslady for help, but she found a dress she loved. When she finally found shoes to go with it she went back to the store where she bought the dress to show her the final product. The saleslady was almost as happy as Lisa and she walked away feeling happy, if not still a little lonely.

Two evenings later, she was the best dressed person on the bus. Underneath a black fake leather jacket that she had bought on impulse during her workwear shopping trip, she was wearing a short sleeve royal blue dress with the first pair of heels she had ever owned. The dress had an asymmetrical neckline and a thin gold belt and ended just above her knees. She took the time to style her hair down—something she never did when waitressing or cleaning. Paired with gold jewelry that she had bought as part of her work outfits she was surprised by the reflection she saw when she looked in the mirror. She wasn't a dull, plain girl trying to blend into the background. Now, she was a confident, intelligent woman with smart clothes and a kickin' bank account.

She walked up to the restaurant as Janet arrived, and Janet nearly passed by without recognizing her. When she realized it was Lisa, her face broke into the biggest smile.

"Lisa! You look stunning!"

"Hi Janet! Thank you! It's a credit to you for telling me that my image mattered."

Once they were at their table, Lisa had to ask, "So, how long does it take to get used to wearing heels? I can already feel my feet starting to hurt!"

"Forever! Just be glad that bookkeepers spend most of their time sitting!"

Manuel and Betsy joined them, and Lisa said a silent thank you to Chad for exposing her to so many restaurants when she first moved to the city. At least she knew how to handle herself, and she could focus on enjoying the time with her guests.

Once they had their drinks and had ordered, they surprised Lisa with gifts. Janet gave her an elegant pen that looked very expensive, "You'll pull that pen out more often than you think!"

And Betsy and Manuel gave her a beautiful gold bracelet with a delicate leaf motif engraved around it. "We've seen you grow so much in the past year and a half," Betsy explained, "And we know you'll continue to grow!" Lisa thanked them and put it on right away.

Over dinner Lisa enjoyed getting to know them all better. She loved hearing stories about people who came from nothing to create successful lives, and all three had done that. In many ways, she felt like her own story was already well on its way, too. After all, here she was in a nice restaurant dressed to perfection with three kind and successful people she could call friends.

The talk turned to Lisa's plans for the future. Now that she had her certificate, she was ready to start applying for jobs. Janet promised to email her the names of a few companies who might be hiring, and Manuel and Betsy said they'd keep their ears open for any possibilities. They encouraged her to send resumes *and* go in person as often as possible, and Betsy suggested she send a thank you email after every interview, even if she didn't get the job. "It's always good to show that you're thoughtful and organized."

By the time they were ready to go, Lisa couldn't wait to start applying for jobs. And both Janet and Manuel's attempts to pay for the meal were thwarted by her earlier planning. Although they protested that she shouldn't have to pay to celebrate her own graduation, Lisa insisted. She did compromise by agreeing to let Manuel and Betsy drive her home instead of taking the bus.

When Lisa walked in the door after one of the nicest evenings of her life, she was confronted with the realities of her living situation.

Somehow, since she left for dinner, the house had gained a new tenant.

A guy with greasy long blonde hair was sitting on the couch with a beer in one hand and a piece of pizza in the other. He was wearing stained sweatpants and a t-shirt with some sort of faded logo on it. His bare feet were on the footstool and the box of pizza sat open on the couch.

Above the blaring TV, he shouted, "Hey babe! Wanna pizza?"

Lisa shook her head and turned away. The TV wasn't loud enough to hide a low whistle from him as she left the room. There were already dirty dishes on the counter, and when she walked into the bathroom her makeup bag was moved to the floor and replaced with a wireless speaker and a shaver.

She quickly washed her face and brushed her teeth and then gathered up everything that was hers in the bathroom and moved it to her room. The last thing she wanted was her towel or toothbrush being touched by that guy. It looked like her days of having great roommates were over.

The next morning Lisa went to grab a yogurt for breakfast, only to find it was already gone. She didn't have much in the fridge, but her new roommate had already dug in. After she went to the laundromat, she'd have to buy food she could keep in her room again.

It wasn't until she had brought back her clean laundry and gone out again for groceries that she came back to face her new roommate. He was sitting at the table wearing nothing but a pair of loose boxer shorts.

"Hey babe! What's up?"

Without smiling, she looked him straight in the eye. "My name's Lisa. You can call me that if you want to talk to me."

"I'm Matt." Looking at the grocery bag still in her hand, "You got anything good in there? I'm starving."

"This is my food. The grocery store is just down the street, though."
She turned and went to her room, her appetite gone after seeing
Matt in his underwear.

Pulling out her notebook and starting up her laptop, she looked at
her numbers. The TV blaring interrupted her almost right away.
She'd have to get some headphones if she didn't want to listen to the
sounds of action movies and hockey games whenever she was home.
Hopefully Matt had a job and wouldn't be around much.

Turning back to her numbers, she smiled despite her current living
conditions. Even with buying a new wardrobe and paying for a
really nice dinner she had over $32,000 in her savings. According to
Ms. Morgan at the bank, this was enough for 10% down on a house,
but only if her 'household' salary was above $83,000. Once she had a
full-time bookkeeping job, she would make an appointment with a
loans officer at the bank to find out for certain when she could
qualify for a mortgage. Her new roommate situation only gave her
more motivation to get her own place.

Lisa spent the rest of the day in her room, applying for the few jobs
she found online, and looking at real estate listings. When supper
time came, she grabbed the home décor magazine she had picked up
at the grocery store and went out to McDonald's to eat. She delayed
going home for as long as possible, hoping to avoid Matt. She sent
her former roommates an SOS about the new roommate, begging
them to come back. All sent sympathetic responses.

CHAPTER 18

Lisa was startled awake by banging on her bedroom door. "What?" She mumbled. Looking at her phone it was five am.

"You got a towel I can use?"

She couldn't believe it. "Matt, get lost."

"Whatever babe."

She lay in bed until she heard a horn honk outside and then the front door slam. Well, she was awake now. She couldn't believe anyone could be so obnoxious. But she didn't need to spend much time at the house so she'd just stay away as much as possible.

Trying to ignore the mess Matt left in the bathroom she quickly showered and got ready for her day. At least she was back to full-time cleaning at the office building. Marco had been a great part-time worker, but he had a full-time summer landscaping job he was starting as soon as school was out. He offered to be available if Lisa ever needed help in the future though, which she appreciated.

Just in case Matt was back in the afternoon, Lisa took everything with her she needed for the day. She'd change at the restaurant and head straight to the offices without stopping at home like she had done in the past. Somehow, she'd survive the new living arrangements. During her lunch break she checked her emails and was pleased to see that one of the jobs she had applied for wanted to schedule an interview. She called the contact name, and set-up an appointment for Thursday at three. That way she could still work at the restaurant and catch her cleaning job after the interview.

There was also an email from Janet, thanking Lisa for dinner and listing four different companies that were looking for a bookkeeper. Lisa arranged with her manager to leave earlier the next day so she could head downtown and drop off resumes. She didn't want to miss a single opportunity.

By Friday Lisa had avoided Matt completely and could sleep through his early morning noise. At least he wasn't banging on her door at five am any more. Saturday she slept in and then went to get her laundry done. When she got back Matt was at the table with what looked like the same pair of boxer shorts on and nothing else.

"Hey babe— "he started, but Lisa cut him off.

"Don't call me babe. If you can't remember that my name is Lisa you don't need to talk to me." She turned to walk away just as the landlord walked in with a younger-looking girl and an older lady behind her.

"Hi Lisa" he started, "This is Amy and her mom, Amy's going to be moving in."

Amy was taller than Lisa, thin, with short blonde hair. She smiled broadly at Lisa and her whole face lit up. Lisa immediately felt like they could be friends.

She started to say hello, but the mom interrupted.

"What's this?" she demanded, gesturing towards Matt. Lisa gave Amy a sympathetic look and stepped as far back as she could without leaving the room.

"Oh—" the landlord faltered, "Well, this is Matt. He just moved in too…"

"And this place is disgusting! You advertised a clean house with mature students. This is unacceptable! There's no way I'm letting my daughter stay in a place with guys hanging around like that. Let's go, Amy!"

"Wait! Just a minute! Matt, you can get dressed, right? And Lisa, I'm sure you were about ready to clean up."

Lisa didn't try to hide how annoyed she was, "Actually, this is the second time I've seen Matt hanging around barely dressed. And I won't clean up after him. This mess is just from him living here a week." Looking at Amy and her mom, Lisa continued, "You don't want to see the bathroom." She turned back to the landlord. "Perhaps Amy is a better candidate than Matt. I'm sure you don't want to see what he can do to your place long-term."

"Babe! I mean, Lisa!" Matt whined.

"And I would appreciate not being harassed by him anymore." Now she looked straight at the landlord. She suddenly realized that it wasn't worth it to stay there if she had to put up with someone like Matt. If she needed to use some of her resources to get a different place, she would.

The landlord looked back at Amy's Mom. "If he's not here anymore will Amy still move in?"

"Not if it looks like this!"

"Oh, don't worry, Lisa will get it all nice and clean for you."

"No, I won't. If you want this place cleaned up, *you'll* have to take care of it. And I won't be staying if he's the type of person you choose to rent out to." Lisa stepped closer to Amy and her mom. Now that she had another voice backing her up, she felt more confident.

"All right all right. Matt, you're out. I'll be back at five to make sure you're gone and the house is clean. If it's not, you won't be getting the damage deposit back."

Matt glared at them before getting up and storming to his room. His boxers slipped down as he went, giving everyone a disgusting last view of his back end.

Lisa turned to Amy, "It's actually a really nice place and a safe neighborhood. I'd love to have you as a roommate if you're still interested. The last people who lived here were great!"

Amy looked at her mom. "Mom?"

Her mom sighed. "I did want you to live near your aunt, and this is the only place that seemed suitable..." She looked at the landlord. "We'll be back at ten tomorrow morning. If the place is clean, we'll take it. Come on, Amy."

After they left, Lisa looked at the landlord. "It may be a good idea to call a cleaning company right away. I don't think Matt's cleaning will meet her standards."

He looked at her thoughtfully. "What's it worth for you to clean it?"

She laughed, "What's it worth to you to have it done right? Remember, Amy's mom will be back tomorrow morning, and I'm not interested in cleaning until Matt's gone."

"One hundred?"

"Two hundred" she countered, "Cash."

"One fifty cash and I'll be more careful who I let in the house."

"Deal. And thank you. This past week has been challenging and I'd like it if we didn't have a repeat."

The landlord stopped short of apologizing, but Lisa was happy with their agreement. She took her clean laundry to her room and locked the door again before going out for a walk. She didn't want to be in the house until Matt was gone. "Call me when you get his keys

THE COST OF CARING

back," She asked as she left. It was up to the landlord now, but if he didn't get rid of Matt, he'd be losing Lisa, Amy, and a clean house.

An hour later Lisa's phone rang. "He's gone. I'll bring you the cash tomorrow at ten. And next time if you think there's a problem just call right away." Lisa figured the last statement was a hidden compliment to her and her judgment. She clearly remembered what he told her before she moved in, "I don't deal with any problems you might have with the roommates. Figure it out yourself."

She turned around and headed back to the house, making one stop at the grocery store to buy some food, heavy duty cleaner, and rubber gloves. At least she had something to do for the day, and she didn't need to avoid the house for the rest of the weekend.

It was early evening when Lisa felt the house was clean enough to pass Amy's mom's inspection. She wasn't sure how things would work out if the lady was planning on spending a lot of time at the house—she certainly came across as the hovering parent type—but anything was better than sharing a house with someone like Matt.

The next morning Lisa enjoyed the luxury of showering in a clean bathroom and eating breakfast at the table without being interrupted. Shortly before ten, she got a call from the restaurant asking if she could come in to cover lunch, since one of the other waitresses hadn't shown up. She agreed to come at eleven.

When the landlord returned with Amy and her mom, the conversation was entirely different from the day before. The state of the house was now acceptable, and Amy would be 'allowed' to stay. Lisa kept her mouth shut when the landlord quoted $600 for rent. She knew no one had paid that much before, but figured it was up to him what he charged. Amy's mom wrote out checks for him and told Lisa they would be back later to move in Amy's things. Again, she kept quiet except to tell Amy she was happy to have her around. It seemed like Amy's mom expected Lisa to be involved with the move, but Lisa wasn't interested in making the lady happy. She'd be living with Amy, not her mom.

The restaurant was busy, and Lisa ended up staying until the dinner rush was over. By the time she got home, she was ready to get into her pajamas and flip through a magazine or two before going to sleep. She said hello to Amy and her mom who were putting some groceries away and slipped into her room. Tomorrow was soon enough to warn Amy about leaving food in the kitchen when other people moved in.

At least between the cash from her landlord and her extra tips she had another $200 to put in savings. Everything helped, but Lisa wished she could move faster towards finally having her own house where she'd have full say about who she lived with.

CHAPTER 19

When Lisa got up, she already had an email waiting with a request for an interview. While she was replying, her phone rang. The company that interviewed her on Thursday wanted to offer her a job. She thanked them for the offer and promised to give them an answer by Wednesday. It was an entry-level job that she was more than qualified for after completing her certificate, but she was a little disappointed at the starting salary. $20,000 was better than she made at the restaurant, but much lower than her ideal starting salary of $30,000.

Janet had already confirmed that she should be able to find a job for at least $26,000 to start. Lisa knew that she would work hard to get raises and hopefully move up the salary ladder but starting too low would leave her a lot more of a wait to get her salary high enough to qualify for a mortgage. She left for her shift at the restaurant hoping something better would turn up, and by lunchtime she had another interview lined up for the next day.

Lisa had warned her boss that she'd eventually be leaving the restaurant for a bookkeeping job, but he was unhappy about losing her and gave her a hard time about leaving early for another interview. She wanted to leave on good terms with him, but she wouldn't give up a chance for an interview just to make him happy.

When she came home in the afternoon to change before her interview, Amy and her mom were sitting at the kitchen table.

"Lisa," Amy's mom started, "Come join us for a cup of tea!"

Lisa had to smile inside at this lady inviting her for tea in the house she lived in, but she didn't want to be rude.

"Oh, I'm sorry, I don't remember your name. Sandra? Right. Sorry, Sandra. I'd love a cup of tea, but I need to change and catch the bus downtown for an interview. Maybe another time!"

"What's the interview for?" Amy asked.

"It's for a bookkeeping position. I just got my certificate in bookkeeping last month and now I'm trying to find a full-time job."

"Don't you work right now?" This from Sandra.

"Yep! I work at the restaurant down the street during the day, and I have a job as a night janitor at an office building Monday to Friday."

"That's why you're never around!"

"Right, and I'd better get going if I'm going to be on time. Have a nice afternoon!"

Lisa enjoyed another chance to try out her new wardrobe. For her interview, she chose her gray dress pants with a white short-sleeve blouse and a red blazer that was light enough to be comfortable in June. She finished it with ankle boots and her gold jewelry. It was encouraging to already have another interview, and she said a mental thank you to Janet for pushing her to find a professional look.

When she came back home that night after cleaning, the house was quiet but Lisa could see a bit of light from under Amy's door. Thinking back to her own first nights at the house, she wished for Amy a more settled experience. No doubt her mom made sure she had bedding and towels before leaving!

The next morning Lisa decided that she could afford to wait for a better offer, so she called back the first company and declined. When asked if she would reconsider, Lisa named a starting salary of $26,000 that she felt would fit her training and work ethic. The lady on the other end stated that the wage wasn't negotiable, even though she personally thought it was too low. She wished Lisa the best before saying goodbye.

Lisa only waited one more day for the phone call she was hoping for. The second company who had interviewed her wanted to offer her a position as an Accounts Receivable/Payable Clerk. The starting wage was $28,000 and Lisa was delighted with the offer. She agreed to come in the next day to sign the paperwork, and she would officially start in two weeks at the beginning of July.

Taking a minute, she sent a quick email to Betsy and Janet to tell them she had a job. For the rest of her shift at the restaurant, Lisa found her mind wandering to the future. It surprised her that she was excited to be able to quit waitressing. She had loved it for the past years, but now she was so happy to be moving on to something else. Once she signed all the papers for her new job, she'd give her notice at the restaurant. Of course, she still had to ask to leave early one more time so she could make her two pm appointment. In exchange she agreed to work Saturday morning for three hours. Technically she was supposed to get a minimum of four hours in a day, but she didn't want to make a stink when she was so close to leaving.

Lisa wore her interview outfit for signing papers but traded the red blazer for a yellow scarf and her leather jacket. She spent the next hour in their Human Resources department, filling out everything from tax forms to a Non-Disclosure Agreement, but she really couldn't imagine any 'secrets' that someone in her position might share with others! She planned to give this job her very best and not to do anything to jeopardize it. After she finished, she left her new workplace with a handful of papers from HR and a definite spring in her step.

With some time to kill she bought a coffee and wandered through downtown for a while. It was exciting to think that she would soon be a part of it. Dressed in her new clothes with her new job just ahead of her she felt quite excited.

Over the weekend Lisa gave her notice to the manager at the restaurant and went to a movie with Amy. It was the first time they could have a conversation without her mom there. She told Lisa that she had to move out of her mom's apartment because her sister had gotten pregnant and needed to move back in. With only two bedrooms there wasn't room for Amy anymore.

Lisa was intrigued by the dynamics Amy described. It sounded like their mom did a lot for her and her sister (including paying Amy's rent) but insisted on having a say in everything the girls did. Her sister's pregnancy was *not* in her mom's plans so there was a lot of tension between them right now.

Amy worked part-time as a care aide at a nursing home, and part-time for her aunt who was in her nineties but still living in her own home. Her dream was to become a nurse, but her mom didn't approve. Sandra was hoping a stint doing personal care would cure her of her ideas, but Amy admitted she really loved her work and was even more determined to stay in health care. Lisa couldn't imagine having to take care of people for a living, but admired Amy for her dedication to her job.

On Monday Lisa was happy to see that her manager had gotten over his grumpiness at her leaving. He asked if she might be available on the weekends, but Lisa was firm. It was time to move on.

Her final shift at the end of the week seemed to last forever, and she found herself watching the clock every time she went back into the kitchen. When it was finally time to leave, she felt like she was closing the door on one chapter in her life and opening another one.

CHAPTER 20

Lisa walked into the office carrying a latte in one hand and her lunch in the other. Today was the second anniversary of her first day at the firm and she was celebrating by buying herself a coffee—a rare splurge. When she got to her desk, she could see that her day would not go unnoticed. A big helium balloon floated above her desk with 'Happy Anniversary' on it.

She planted a smile on her face and looked around for Sarah. Sure enough, the second floor receptionist was peaking around the corner to see Lisa's expression. "Hi Sarah! I guess this is your doing."

"Ooooh, how did you guess? Happy anniversary Lisa! Do you want to go out for lunch? My treat!"

Lisa held up her lunch bag. "No thanks, I'm going to stick around for lunch. Thanks for the balloon!" She moved the balloon to the side and turned on her monitor. Although she was polite to Sarah, she had learned not to give her any encouragement. That girl was desperate to be Lisa's best friend, but more than five minutes with her left Lisa feeling drained. She just couldn't handle bubbly and fake.

Other than Sarah, Lisa loved her job. Her hard work and loyalty were paying off. She was now the Head of Accounts Receivable/Payable for Golden Lion Investments, a commercial real estate company. When she started, there was a sudden round of people quitting, and it was the owner's wife who trained Lisa because the other senior people were either gone or too busy filling in for those who had left.

As a result, the owner heard firsthand from his wife everything about Lisa, and after just eighteen months she received a promotion that most people waited decades for. The new responsibilities left her unable to continue her janitor job, and she passed the full contract onto Freddy, who was now studying business management part-time.

Even with a big raise, she continued to be careful about her spending. Most days she made her own coffee at home for the bus ride to work (using a little coffee maker that sat on her dresser), bought a simple lunch at the discount grocery store around the corner, and shopped the sales to keep her business wardrobe up-to-date.

Lisa found the job challenging every day. As always, the accounting part was the easiest. But learning to deal with others was a huge learning curve. When she was promoted, they sent her for a one-week training seminar in Florida to prepare her for the increased management responsibilities she would have. It was her first time flying, her first time staying overnight in a hotel, and her first time wearing shorts and a tank top outside in January!

She was learning to navigate office politics without getting involved, and with her example the department was starting to work as a team, rather than a group of individuals always trying to one-up each other. She also worked hard to change the company policy of always paying invoices thirty days past due. It had been done for so many years that everyone just accepted it. Lisa spent three weekends coming in to work and totaling all the late fees and interest they had paid over the years, and then showing what that money could have earned if they had invested it in property. The numbers were eye-

THE COST OF CARING

watering. One month later all invoices were up-to-date, and they had not fallen behind since.

Lisa earned high praise from the CFO for creating the new policy and implementing it. She thought he could have done the same thing she did with the numbers and saved the company from leaking money for so many years, but she kept that thought to herself.

Another new job she gave herself was chasing down accounts that were in arrears. Many of these had just been written off as bad debts in the past, but Lisa was determined to close this expensive way of dealing with the problem. She invited Janet out for Sunday brunch and asked for her advice. Janet was surprised that such a huge corporation was letting tenants get away with non-payment and agreed with Lisa that she could do something about it.

Lisa visited the offices in person that were behind on their lease payments. Used to ignoring phone calls and letters, many of these businesses didn't know what to do when they were face-to-face with Lisa. Those who still didn't bring their accounts up to date were immediately faced with legal action, and within a few short months many of their tenants who had been behind were completely caught up. Plus, word spread through their buildings that the new lady in Accounting meant business!

While she earned respect and promotions at work, she was still working hard to qualify for a mortgage at a good rate. At first, the bank wanted to see two full years of income from her janitor job before they would accept it as income because they treated it differently than a salaried job. Then, she was told that she didn't have a high enough credit rating. Even though she used her credit card monthly, and always paid it in full, she had not taken out a loan for anything—which made her look like a credit risk!

The bank told her to take out a loan for a car, or even just a loan for any reason so she could build up credit by paying it back on time, but she just didn't feel comfortable getting into debt, even for a 'good' cause.

Lisa didn't check her personal finances spreadsheet as often as she used to. She knew she still needed higher income to qualify for a good mortgage from the bank. Her salary was now at $48,000 and in her new role she would qualify for a bonus at the end of the year, which would help to bump up her total income.

After leaving the janitor job, she switched to looking for book-keeping work she could do online in the evenings and weekends to help boost her income. Using a freelancing platform, she slowly built up a good reputation and regular jobs, and this month she would clear $1,000 after fees paid to the platform. Unfortunately, this was considered 'contract' work, and counted less in her mortgage application than a traditional job.

While her $84,000 in savings should have been enough to prove she could handle a mortgage, it wasn't enough to get her the low interest rate she wanted. But by the new year with her increased salary she was confident she'd finally be house shopping for real.

She got used to seeing co-workers jet off for exotic vacations, only to complain for months afterward about how broke they were. And those who spent money on cars, insurance, and parking were the most likely to show up late whenever there were traffic problems. Her own life wasn't exactly exciting all the time, but it was secure, and she knew enough single women at the office who were really struggling financially to know how good she had it.

Over the summer Lisa continued to put in long days at work, and then spend at least part of the time in the evenings and on the weekends building up her freelance work. She loved the freedom it gave her to choose interesting clients and earn extra money without leaving the house. One of her roommates who was studying journalism followed Lisa's lead and was using the same platform to pick up writing jobs while she put herself through university. Lisa had quickly connected with Julia when she moved in a year ago. Just like her, Julia was on her own and didn't have the bank of dad and mom to rely on, like nearly everyone else seemed to do. They often ended up working at the kitchen table when everyone else was out partying.

Different roommates continued to come and go over the past two years, but they were pretty much all decent. Only once Lisa had called the landlord when a roommate was obviously dealing drugs and she was gone the next day. Other than that, it was as good as it could be. She kept in contact with Amy, who now lived with her aunt so she could care for her full-time. Amy had not started nursing school yet, but she was happy caring for her aunt in the meantime.

The original roommates still kept in touch and would meet Lisa for dinner whenever they were in the area. Mark was in grad school on a research grant. Jennifer and Collette were both registered nurses, and Jennifer was spending a year volunteering at a hospital in Chile. Chad was now working at his dad's business and had resigned himself to taking over when he retired. They were all impressed with Lisa's meteoric rise at Golden Lion, and she loved it when she was the one to pay for them when they went out for dinner. A few years ago, she sure couldn't have done that!

Lisa finished her 'Anniversary Day' at work without any further balloons or invitations.

Amy had invited Lisa to come over for supper at her aunt's, so she went straight there. Amy's Aunt Helena was a corporate secretary until she retired, and she loved her niece's friend who knew how to 'dress properly' for work. Today Lisa was wearing a gray pencil skirt with a short-sleeve rose colored blouse, nude heels, and a gray blazer. Even though it was warm out, the office's air conditioning required a blazer or cardigan year-round.

The smell of roast beef met Lisa before she even came in the door. Aunt Helena had been coaching Amy in the kitchen, and she loved the chance to learn to cook—something her own mom had never done. Aunt Helena was really her great aunt, and she and Amy were very close. Without Amy's live-in care she would have been in a care home long ago, but with Amy she could stay in her own home.

Lisa wasn't surprised to see Amy's mom sitting at the dining room table with Aunt Helena. After she said hello to the elderly lady and kissed her cheek she turned to Sandra, "Hello, Sandra. How are you doing?" She heard from Amy that Sandra was much more relaxed since becoming a grandma but seemed to spend more and more time at Aunt Helena's now that little Connor was learning to talk and run around. He sounded like a handful!

"Hi Lisa, I'm good thank you. Just enjoying adult conversation that isn't interrupted by Connor! I was in the neighborhood to see a potential client and thought I'd stop by." She looked at Aunt Helena, "If I had known Amy's cooking skills had improved this much, I would have started coming over every night!"

"You might want to wait until you try the food Mom!" Amy called from the kitchen.

"What do you do for work?" Lisa asked. She knew Sandra did something that involved evening and weekend work, and she must be doing OK to support her daughters.

"I'm a mortgage broker."

"Is that the same as the loans officer at the bank?"

"Yes and no. I do help people with mortgages, but I have access to a full range of mortgage companies, not just one bank. I take each client's unique circumstances and find them the best mortgage." Amy started bringing in dishes and placing them on the table. The smell of roast beef, mashed potatoes, gravy, and glazed carrots was mouthwatering.

Once everyone was enjoying their food, Lisa continued the conversation with Sandra. "Do you charge a fee?"

"No, there's no cost to the client. Mortgage companies pay me a commission whenever a successful transaction is completed for a client."

"Maybe you can help me. I've been trying to qualify for a mortgage for over a year now, but my bank says that my salary isn't high enough yet. And I don't have anyone who can co-sign for me. Well, even if I did, you would think a fully employed woman with a down payment saved up could buy a house on her own!"

"Atta girl!" Aunt Helena joined in, "You do it on your own. And if you get married, you keep the house in your name!" While Aunt Helena was one of the first women in her family to work full-time, she was also one of the first to get divorced. Amy told Lisa that she had represented herself in court when her ex-husband tried to claim her assets—and won.

"I specialize in unique situations. I'd be interested in working with you." They agreed to meet back at Aunt Helena's the next morning to go over the specifics. Sandra typically met in client's homes, but they agreed that Lisa's house would be less than ideal with everyone coming and going.

For the rest of dinner they talked about Aunt Helena's favorite subject—her years working as an executive secretary to an oil company CEO. It was always fun to listen to her, and it reminded Lisa to be grateful for progress in women's equality in the workplace. Sure, they still had a ways to go, but Lisa didn't have to worry about getting fired if she stopped wearing heels to work, or if she filed a complaint against a co-worker.

CHAPTER 21

The next morning Lisa was back at Aunt Helena's with her most recent credit report, her savings account statement, her proof of employment and salary, and her statements from the freelancing work. Fortunately, she could use a printer at work when needed, and she had her statements until the end of June already printed. She wasn't sure what else to bring.

It only took Sandra a few minutes to look over her documents. "Is there anything else you have related to your finances? Any debts or loans?"

"No, this is it. I've had my credit card for four years now and I pay it in full every month."

"Well, this is impressive Lisa!"

"It is? I mean, thank you! But the bank kept telling me I didn't have enough borrowing history, so I thought maybe I wasn't doing so well."

"Your ability to budget and save is really astounding. I have access to lenders that would fall over themselves to give you a mortgage."

"But what kind of rate could I get? I want to pay off my mortgage as soon as possible and pay as little interest as I can get away with."

"I'm confident I can get you a good rate. If you'd like me to work for you, I'll have you sign this agreement. Then in about a week we can meet again, and I can show you all your options. It would be a pleasure to help you buy your first home. And that's something else. As a first home buyer, there are some incentives that will help out."

Lisa felt a flicker of excitement start to grow, "How long until I can start looking for houses?"

"Well, you can start any time, but many sellers prefer buyers who are already pre-approved. I can contact you midweek with some preliminary numbers about what you will qualify for. Full pre-approval takes about ten days though."

"I've been waiting four years, so I can wait another ten days. Thank you so much Sandra!"

They signed an agreement, and Sandra promised to copy all the documents and bring them back to Aunt Helena's for Lisa to pick up. The four women spent the rest of the morning chatting about the different things Lisa might want in a house. For Lisa, it was the closest she had been to making her dream come true and she could hardly contain herself.

Sunday morning, she took the bus to a new subdivision that was advertised in the papers. It was the first weekend that their show homes were open, and Lisa wanted to look through them. She didn't plan on buying a new home, but she wanted to see and touch something real. Looking through real estate listings online was still interesting, but now Lisa wanted something she could get a real feel for.

Expecting a crowd of people, she was surprised that only a handful were walking through the four houses on display. From the talk at work she knew that commercial real estate was slowing down this year. Maybe residential was in the same situation.

The show homes were beautiful in the way that a store window display was beautiful—interesting to look at, but without much substance. She quickly realized how little she knew about houses. What was the big deal about granite countertops and stainless steel kitchen appliances? She'd be happy with a kitchen she could leave her food in without it getting snatched! And a second washer/dryer in the master suite? Did people need to do that much laundry in a week?

Her other questions involved trying to turn the house into a boarding house. She hadn't thought out how that might actually work. It seemed like unnecessary work to buy a new, finished house and then change it right away. What she wanted was a big old house with lots of bedrooms that needed work, so she could turn it into exactly what she wanted—once she figured out what she wanted!

Instead of going straight home, she went to one of the parks in the city, bought a freshly squeezed lemonade and walked around the lake. The park was full of families playing, teenagers flirting, and young adults tossing frisbees and footballs. She loved the city and the way people always took advantage of the good weather to get out in the sun. Admittedly, she didn't spend enough time enjoying what she had access to.

Riding the bus home, she decided two things: she needed to enjoy more of the simple things that the city offered, and she needed to spend a lot of time figuring out what she needed to make a house a boarding house.

Just as she was getting off the bus, her phone rang. Answering it, she received the news that would completely turn her life upside down. It was her mom.

"Your dad collapsed at work this morning and he's been rushed to the hospital."

Lisa's first reaction was total indifference. "OK… where are you?"

"I'm at home. I think the hospital's supposed to call with an update after they get him checked out."

"Well, thanks for letting me know. Feel free to call again when you hear something."

After she hung up, Lisa went about her Sunday evening routine of choosing her outfits for the week and reviewing the major work tasks she needed to get done. She rarely went into the office over the weekend, but she liked to have a plan at the start of each week.

Her thoughts wandered to her parents. She was less concerned about her dad's recovery than she was about all she had lost growing up with him. It was hard to ignore how dysfunctional their little family was when she saw the interactions between her roommates and their parents. They were always calling their parents to ask for advice, help, or money. And when parents dropped by to check on their kids, they were so concerned that everything was OK for them.

Lisa's dad didn't even care that she was on her own, except that it meant she wasn't at home paying *him* rent. She had put some effort into letting go of the resentment she felt about how she was raised, even taking advantage of a program offered at work for life coaching. What she learned was that her parent's choices impacted her but were not her fault or her responsibility. They had chosen how to treat her, and she could either be resentful or she could focus on her own choices and future.

Her mom didn't call again until Monday. When Lisa checked the voicemail at lunchtime, she heard the words that would change everything, "He's gone Lisa. Last night your dad died. I don't know what to do. Please come home."

Lisa contacted the only funeral home in her home town before calling her mom back. Part of her didn't want to talk to her mom yet, and part of her wanted to confirm that he was really dead. They already had her dad's body but had not received any instructions from her mom.

The discussion with her mom — when she forced herself to call back — was difficult. She seemed unable to make a single decision, but Lisa figured maybe she was in shock and grieving. They agreed that he should be cremated, and Lisa called back the funeral home and used her credit card to pay for a simple service on Thursday followed by a cremation. She promised her mom she'd arrive early in the morning on Thursday and go to the funeral home with her.

That evening as Lisa pulled out the only dress suitable for a funeral, Sandra called. Lisa realized that she hadn't even called her friends to tell them what was happening. She gave Sandra a brief update and agreed to call again when she was back in the city. Then she had a few restless days and nights before the unpleasant task of going to her dad's funeral could be over. Early Thursday morning she got on a bus heading to the town she had sworn she'd never go back to.

CHAPTER 22

It was two in the morning when Lisa finished telling her mom about the past four years. Not one to ever stay up this late, Lisa was exhausted, but somehow peaceful too. She hadn't realized how much she had wanted to talk about her life. Her mom looked at her and gave her a sad smile.

"I'm so proud of you. I know you did everything on your own and I didn't help you at all, but I'm so, *so* proud of you."

"Thanks Mom. And thanks for asking to hear my story. There were so many times when I wanted to call and talk to you. I'm glad I got to tell you everything. Do you think you can fall asleep now? It's two am…"

"That's about the time I usually fall asleep."

"Goodnight Mom."

"Goodnight dear."

The next morning Lisa focused on getting her and her mom out of the house. She wanted to close the door on their past and get back to the job and the friends that she had grown to love in the past four years. Over the last few days she had received supportive text messages or voicemails from everyone as word spread that her dad had passed away. She hadn't returned any yet, but knowing they were thinking about her made everything a little easier.

It felt good to get dressed in her own clothes again—the clothes that reflected the changes she had made in her life. She still wore jeans on her days off, but they were usually blue now, and always paired with a fun blouse or dressy t-shirt and a cute pair of boots. After a quick cup of coffee, she started packing the things in the kitchen that they were keeping. Since they would have their own kitchen as soon as they moved back to the city, these things would go a long way to getting set up.

At eight am she went to wake up her mom and give her some time to get up slowly. She was learning that her mom did best in the morning when she could slowly shift from sitting to standing to getting ready.

By nine they were both eating breakfast and planning the day. Lisa wanted to finish up everything at the house as soon as possible, but she didn't want to push her mom too much. It was challenging to have to keep someone else's needs in mind after spending years only focusing on her own needs.

However, her mom made it easier when she asked, "How soon can we move to your new place?"

Lisa smiled. "Well, we need to finish going through the house, pack everything we want to keep, get rid of everything else, and get the house and yard cleaned up. Oh! And list the house! Do you have a real estate agent you want to use?"

"The neighbor down the street is a real estate agent. At least, I think she is. I've never met her, but she drives a car that has a real estate logo on it." Maria could even quote the name of the company and the lady. After a quick phone search, Lisa dialed her number.

"Hi, my name is Lisa Naylor. My parents live in number 14, just down the street from you... Thank you, yes it was quite unexpected.

My mom needs to sell the house as soon as possible, but hopefully for a good price. Is this something you could help us with?... Yes, that would be fine. We'll see you at one today. Thanks very much!"

Lisa hung up and looked at her mom. "She'll be here at one. I have no idea what's involved in selling a house. But in the meantime, we can keep working on cleaning things out. Once we've met with her, we'll know more. Then I'll book a moving truck to take the things we're keeping, and we'll say goodbye to this house."

Maria reached across the table and hugged Lisa, "Last week I thought my life was done, and now I'm so excited! You're a good girl Lisa!"

"Thanks!... Um, I'd like to keep any of the tools in the garage that I can use when I buy a house. I don't suppose you know what's out there?"

"I have no idea! But I think the man across the street does a lot of work on his house. Maybe he knows?"

"Great idea! I'll head over there now and ask him. While I'm out, do you think you could go through Dad's things in your bedroom, just to make sure everything can go to the thrift store? I might have time to take a load over before the real estate lady comes."

"I think I can manage that. You go see the neighbor, I'll clean up here."

Ten minutes later, Lisa was in the garage with the neighbor — a man who looked to be around Lisa's age, and introduced himself as Jesse Hendricks. He had moved in after she left home, so she had never met him — and it wasn't like her parents had made any effort to get to know the neighbors.

Apparently, her dad had collected all sorts of tools without any specific project in mind. Jesse showed her which tools would be handy to have when she owned her own home.

"You definitely want a hammer, some screwdrivers, and a wrench.

Oh, and this cordless drill is a Makita—that's a good quality brand. Let's see…Yep, here's the drill bits to go with the drill…And the charger." He grabbed a tool box and put some essentials in it for Lisa.

"There are quite a few other things here that are worth something. What's your plan?"

Lisa paused, "I do want to keep the home improvement tools, but to be honest, I need to generate as much cash as possible. My dad left my mom almost destitute. She'll be lucky if she walks away with the shirt on her back."

He whistled, "Gee, I'm sorry. I wondered, you know. When I first moved in, I could see your mom sitting by the window all the time. I came over to introduce myself and your dad answered the door and told me he wasn't interested before I could say anything. Your mom always looked so lonely sitting there." He looked at Lisa, and she wondered if he was judging her for not visiting.

"My dad was a horrible man. I stayed away from home so I could avoid him, and Mom and I both missed out on time together because of him. But we'll be OK now. I've got an apartment in the city, and she'll be staying with me."

"That's good. My parents are both gone, so I'll risk the cliché and tell you to appreciate the time you have with your mom. Listen, I've got a buddy who's a mechanic, and quite a tool guy. Do you want me to ask him to come over and give you an idea of what this other stuff is worth?"

"Yeah, that'd be great, thank you! I do want to keep the home improvement tools, so that would work out. And while you're being so helpful, do you know of a few guys I can hire to help me load furniture into a moving truck, maybe at the end of the week? I want to get my mom settled in the new place as soon as possible."

"Sure, if it's Friday night or Saturday I can get a few guys together. Buy the beer and pizza and you've got a deal!"

Laughing she put out her hand to shake his. "It's a deal. Thanks Jesse!" They traded phone numbers and Jesse promised to let her know when his mechanic friend could come over. Lisa took a few minutes to look over the home improvement tools Jesse advised her to keep. She hoped one day she'd know how to use them!

There was just enough time to take a car load of donations (including her dad's clothes) to the thrift store before having a quick lunch with her mom so they'd be ready when the real estate agent came over. Her mom found over a hundred dollars in different pockets of her dad's clothes and was quite pleased with herself. "Imagine, me just going in his pockets and taking what I want!"

CHAPTER 23

Kathleen McKinnon, the real estate agent, arrived when they were just finishing lunch. She accepted Lisa's offer of a cup of tea and sat down at the table with them. Although she was dressed for business in a black suit with a blue pinstriped dress shirt under and ridiculously high heels, her sincerity and care came through as soon as she started talking.

When Lisa explained that the house had a second mortgage on it, and there were significant debts that had been left to her mom, Kathleen's bright red lips tightened in a straight line. But a minute later her face softened as she looked at the two women.

"I'll do everything in my power to get you the best price possible. I'm so sorry you're in this situation, but I'll help in any way I can. How do you feel about showing me around?"

One look at her mom and Lisa could see Maria needed to lie down. "Could we start in the master bedroom? Then Mom can lie down while I show you the rest of the house."

Her mom looked relieved. After a quick assessment of the master bedroom, Kathleen stepped out while Lisa made sure her mom was as comfortable as possible. She wondered how many of the pain pills her mom was taking throughout the day. One of the first things to do after they moved was seeing a doctor.

Meeting Kathleen outside the bedroom door, she showed her through the house. She didn't say much until they walked out to the back fence in the yard. There was a gate opening onto the school field, but Lisa's dad had boarded it up a long time ago to stop kids from walking through his yard.

"Not much of a people person, was he?"

Lisa rested her arms on the boards for a minute, looking out onto a past where friends seemed as offensive to her Dad as she was. "Honestly, he was an asshole. There wasn't a day that went by that he didn't tell me what a disappointment I was, but to see what he's done to my mom leaving her in this situation is even worse. I guess it's no surprise we're not really grieving over our loss."

"You sure are different than him. And it's so beautiful how you're getting your mom out of here. I think a fresh start will turn her into a whole new woman! Like I said before, I'll do my best to get you the most I can for your place."

"Do you have any idea how much that might be?"

"Well, you've actually got a lot going for you. This school district has been getting rave reviews for the past couple of years, and people from the city will pay almost anything for a house in the right neighborhood. The house isn't much to look at right now, but it's got good bones and it's been well maintained. I think we can get $360,000 to $390,000 for it, especially if you can offer a quick closing date. With it being the beginning of the summer, buyers will want to move in before the next school year starts."

Lisa was shocked. It seemed crazy that her childhood home full of bad memories could be worth so much. She had thought it would sell for much less. If they could get what Kathleen suggested her mom might just make it out of this mess in one piece.

"When would you be ready to list it?"

"Oh, that depends on you. It sounds like you're taking a lot of furniture with you. That's fine, but I recommend you hire a cleaning crew to come in after everything's out. And it would be helpful to have the home inspection done in advance. That will help motivate buyers to put in an offer. Ideally, I would like to host an open house on a Sunday when people have time to look through the place. That would require getting the photographer in by Thursday so I can advertise in the weekend papers."

Lisa knew a tight deadline would help her power through the last rooms and get everything done. "How about this Sunday? I won't be able to get the furniture out until Friday night, but maybe we could work around the furniture for cleaning and photos?"

Kathleen smiled. "You're a go-getter, just like me. Yes, if you can have the house ready for pictures by Thursday, we can work with what's here. Feel free to move everything you can into the garage — it's not much to look at inside, so I won't put up any pictures of it. You also need to get the lawn mown, and the shrubs trimmed. It's too bad there aren't any flower beds, but I'll bring over some of my own pots of flowers to brighten the front up a bit. Why don't we go back inside and go over the numbers?"

When Lisa checked on her mom, she was fast asleep, so Kathleen left the real estate contract for her to sign. Before she left, she took measurements of all the rooms except the master bedroom and took a few preliminary pictures. She surprised Lisa by reaching out and giving her a gentle hug goodbye. "I'll get this house taken care of. Don't worry about anything!"

Needing to get rid of some excess energy after committing to having the house ready in three days, Lisa decided to take care of the yard. Getting out the lawnmower from the garage, she was relieved that it started on the first try. She remembered being yelled at for not being able to start it when she was younger because she was too weak at thirteen to pull the starter cord. Doing yardwork because it was a choice and not an order was a lot more enjoyable. Two hours

116

later Lisa had the front and back lawn mown and the shrubs tidied up.

Her mom was awake and ready to get up when Lisa came inside. It was nice to share some happy financial news with her about the potential house sale. She agreed that they could have the house cleaned out by Thursday and mentioned again how glad she would be to move. After she signed the contract Lisa returned it to Kathleen's. When she dropped it off Kathleen gave her the names of a few people who would do a good job cleaning the house. She had a landscaper too, but Lisa assured her that was done already. With Lisa's permission, she offered to book a home inspection for Wednesday, if the company she preferred was available.

Jesse came out when she passed by on her way home and said his friend wanted to come that evening. She needed space in the garage to put the furniture they were keeping, so the timing was perfect.

Lisa quickly made sandwiches for supper. In the past few days she had made more meals than the last four years combined. With roommates who always helped themselves to food, Lisa had gotten into the habit of buying a cheap frozen dinner or salad on the way home every night to eat for supper. Now she had the luxury of a kitchen where food didn't go missing, but it was a lot more work, especially since she was keeping her mom fed too.

Her mom offered to tidy up when the doorbell rang. Jesse's friend was there, looking like quite a stereotypical mechanic with long black hair, blue overalls, and grease-stained hands. Jesse introduced him as Joe, and together they walked to the garage.

"Whoa, you've got some good tools here!" Right away he started looking through things, checking connections, moving parts, and other things that had Lisa baffled. "So, you want to get rid of it all, right?"

"Yeah. It's for my mom. She won't exactly be doing any repairs, and she's in a pretty tight financial situation. What do you think of everything?"

"Most of its good quality. I can use a lot of it, and I'd probably sell the rest of it myself. Would you take $1,000 for it all?"

"Um…" Lisa was shocked at the price. "Can you take it all right now? It's just that we need the space."

"Would you take a check?"

"Not a chance!" She smiled to take the edge off. "But there's a bank around the corner that's open late on Mondays."

"Aw, you got me. OK. I'll be back in twenty minutes. Don't sell it when I'm gone!"

"I'll guard it with my life. See you soon Joe!"

Closing the garage door carefully — now she knew there was something worth something in there — she went inside to tell her mom the good news.

"At least that man spent some of his cash on something worthwhile!" Lisa had to agree with her mom.

After Joe had come, paid Lisa, and taken all the tools away, Lisa took some time to wipe down the shelves and sweep out the garage. It looked a lot bigger now, and she thought maybe someone would get use out of this garage in its next life. Just as she was finishing Kathleen texted to confirm the home inspector on Wednesday morning.

That night she slept the sleep of the very hardworking. She was used to long work hours, but the work involved in getting a house ready to sell was a different challenge.

CHAPTER 24

Thursday morning Lisa was up early to get a few hours of freelance work done at the café before her mom woke up. There was lots to do at the house still, and she needed to make sure her client's bookkeeping was taken care of. The past two days had been filled with sorting the rest of the things in the house, making numerous trips to the thrift store (where they greeted her by name now), and hiring a removals company that came to take a load to the dump last night. For someone who always kept track of every penny coming and going from her bank account, Lisa had completely lost track. She was trying to focus on the job at hand, and worry about the money later, but it bothered her that she was less in control of her finances.

Early Saturday morning Jesse and a few friends would show up to help her load the moving truck she had already reserved, which she would drive to their new apartment. Since they were moving in the morning instead of at night, beer and pizza as payment turned into coffee and donuts. Jesse was really good natured about the whole thing, and Lisa was grateful for this new friendly face in her old neighborhood.

Manuel and his sons agreed to meet her at the city end to help unload everything. Again this lovely family was coming through for her and helping out above and beyond what she would have expected from friends.

After the truck was unloaded, she'd have to drive it back to the rental center in town before picking up the car and driving it back to the apartment. It would be a ridiculously long day but she couldn't think of any way to avoid it. Whenever she got overwhelmed she tried to focus on the image of her mom relaxing in their new apartment, away from the toxic memories of their old house.

Work done, submitted, and invoiced, Lisa was back at the house by nine to start helping her mom get up. At the moment she was refusing to acknowledge the extra challenges that her mom's health posed to their plans, but in the back of her mind she was already worrying about how things would work out going forward. It was just so much more work to be responsible for someone else.

While her mom was getting up, Lisa let in the cleaners that Kathleen had recommended. It was a relief to hand off responsibility for cleaning everything to them so she could focus on her mom.

Last night she had struggled through a rather uncomfortable bath time with her mom. Getting her in and out of the tub was scary and she couldn't imagine how her dad had managed. Then there was the added challenge of trying to get her mom's hair washed and rinsed. She didn't know which of them was more embarrassed at the end, but at least her mom was clean. The mental list of things to do at the apartment now included getting a shower seat for the one bathroom and learning how to make sure her mom didn't fall getting in and out of the bath.

When Kathleen arrived with the photographer just after lunch the house was sparkling clean and Lisa was starting to relax. She had packed everything except a few basics like a kettle and enough clothes for the next few days. The excess furniture was already gone. They agreed to keep the beds, two small armchairs, the TV and TV stand, and the kitchen table and chairs, plus the boxes and tools waiting in the garage. Everything else was already picked up by a charity that Kathleen recommended. It was a relief to know they would have less to move to the city, and Lisa hoped they had kept enough to get by.

Kathleen already had a family interested in buying the house, but she planned on running the open house anyway in the hopes of generating a bidding war. The home inspection uncovered some water damage in the master bathroom, but she assured them that it wouldn't impact the price of the house. People were just too willing to buy the house because of the neighborhood. She also brought a half dozen large pots of flowers for the front and back yard and Lisa was amazed at the transformation. She'd never been interested in gardening, but now she was suddenly looking forward to having her very own yard to grow flowers in.

Jesse popped by after work to see if they needed any help. Lisa assured him that they were OK and thanked him again for his help with the tools and the truck loading. It was only after he left that Maria noted that he seemed interested in Lisa. She was shocked at her mom's observations.

"I don't think so Mom. He's just a nice guy. It's too bad you didn't get to know him earlier."

"Lisa, hon, I spend my whole days watching the people along this road. I think I can tell when a man is interested in someone!"

"Well that may be, but *I'm* just not interested. No offense, but I'd hate to end up being married to someone like Dad."

"Oh, I think you'll do better than me. I was so young and naïve when I met your dad, and even though my parents and friends warned me about him I didn't listen. By the time I was your age I was already married and pregnant. You're far ahead of me that way. Even having a good job, and friends. I didn't have any of that, and I thought your dad would take care of all my needs. A girl needs to stand on her own two feet even if she's married. I couldn't."

They sat in quiet for a few minutes before Lisa spoke, "If you could go back and do things differently, what would you do?"

Marie looked into the distance and smiled, "I would be a preschool teacher. I love that age so much. All excited about everything and learning something new every day. I'd love to be surrounded with the energy of those kids!"

Lisa laughed out loud. "You totally surprised me with that one! Preschoolers? Really? They're like terrors on two legs!"

"Oh, not at all! It's the one age when they think everything's possible, before they go to school and get their dreams crushed. I loved my time with you at that age. As soon as Robert left for work and I had you to myself life was perfect. The rest of the time when he was around I was too busy trying to keep you quiet so he didn't yell at you. We missed out on a lot of fun times because of him."

"Huh. Well, maybe we'll move to a neighborhood with lots of preschoolers one day and you can have your fill!"

With that optimistic view of the future, Lisa helped her mom get ready for bed. She planned to let her sleep as long as possible tomorrow, so she'd be ready for the big day on Saturday. Lisa was very grateful that Friday didn't have any extra surprises or demands that popped up. Her mom spent the day resting and Lisa finished packing up the last bits and pieces. They were ready to move!

CHAPTER 25

L isa breathed a sigh of relief when she pulled up at the apartment and saw Manuel, Betsy, and the boys waiting for her. She had never driven something as big as a moving truck, and the drive had been tense. Betsy took one look at Maria and decided they should be friends. She helped her walk to the apartment — Maria was moving quite slowly after the early morning and hour-long ride in the truck. As soon as the two armchairs were unloaded and set up the two ladies settled in for a visit. It didn't take long to unpack the truck, and Manuel insisted on getting the beds set up so Lisa leaver right away to return the truck and pick up the car. Then Lisa was on her way back to her hometown — hopefully for the last time.

The drive gave Lisa time to think about everything that had happened since her dad died almost two weeks ago. She was happy to have her mom with her and to have the chance to build the relationship between them. It was clear now that she had really missed having a mom she could connect with every day, even though she thought she was fine on her own when she had to be.

But there was another part of her that was already feeling a bit desperate and trapped. She couldn't just think about herself and her goals now. She had to think about her mom, and every big decision she made would also impact her mom. It was a lot to put on her shoulders and she wasn't sure she could handle it.

After a quick stop to drop off the rental truck and pick up her car, Lisa was on her way back into the city. She realized she hadn't eaten anything since the breakfast she bought at the café at six that morning but she didn't want to stop for food and delay her arrival at home any longer. Hopefully her mom could get some rest after Manuel set up the beds, even if it was without the sheets and bedding that were packed somewhere. Lisa tried to picture the nearest grocery store to her apartment but her tired brain wouldn't cooperate. She'd just have to figure it out when she got there.

Just after five she parked the car in her new parking spot and dragged herself inside to check on her mom before going to get groceries. She was greeted by Manuel and Betsy sitting at the table with her mom and the delicious aroma of *tapado*—a Central American seafood soup that was just perfect for the end of a busy day. Lisa could have cried for joy.

"We thought we'd eat a little early so your mom could get to bed. You came just in time!" Manuel got up and pulled out the last chair at the table for Lisa as if she was in a fancy restaurant.

"Thank you all *so* much!!"

"Betsy is a firecracker!" her mom bragged. "She's got all the kitchen stuff unpacked, and the beds made, and after she drove the boys home she brought back this delicious food!"

Lisa had to agree, and smiled her thanks to Betsy and Manuel. She was beyond relieved that she didn't have to go out again tonight or try to get beds made before she collapsed into one.

"I also brought over a few things—there's some coffee and tea, and eggs and bread for breakfast tomorrow. You'll have to get some groceries, but at least you can start your day off right."

"Betsy, are you sure you're not an angel dressed up as a human? I've been dreading the thought of having to go out again, and here you've taken care of everything. Thank you!"

"I'm just happy you have your mom here safe and sound. That's the best gift!"

The next morning found Lisa up early and in a rush to get things sorted out before going back to work the next day. Not wanting to wake her mom up, she slipped out of the house and drove to her old room in the city to pick up the last of her things. Technically she had two more weeks, but she didn't like to leave loose ends. After packing up the rest of her things and carrying all her work clothes to the backseat of the car, she paused for a minute and looked around. In her time here she had gone from a frightened and angry girl to a proud, confident, successful woman. It was a transformation she would never forget. She determined that one day she'd help someone else do the same thing.

She stopped at the grocery store near her old house and grabbed enough basics to get them through a few days. The rest of the day would be spent settling into the new apartment and doing some freelance work.

CHAPTER 26

When Lisa arrived at work she was greeted by a beautiful bouquet of flowers and a sympathy card from her co-workers. But she only had a moment to appreciate the sentiment before she was slammed with everything that hadn't been done during the time she was off. For the first time, she took Sarah up on the offer to pick her up something for lunch, and she worked straight through the day.

Normally Lisa would stay late at night to continue to catch up, but she felt obligated to leave at five so her mom wasn't alone any longer. If this was what it felt like to have a partner or kids at home, Lisa sympathized with women everywhere. She made a mental note to be more patient with women in the office when they didn't want to work late. This was a whole new experience for her and she felt bad for not understanding earlier what other women with obligations at home must go through.

Though she'd bought ingredients for dinner the day before, Lisa couldn't be bothered to go home and make it. Instead, she stopped at the trusty downtown market that had been selling her frozen dinners for almost two years and picked up a pre-made dinner.

With a longer bus ride to the apartment she wasn't home until after six, and she could tell her mom was worried. They'd have to figure out how to deal with all that, but not tonight. After eating their dinners, Lisa tried to answer her mom's questions about her day. She understood that she had spent the day sitting and watching TV, and was keen for some conversation, but Lisa would have rather sat in quiet.

She didn't have it in her to tackle her freelance work like she usually did in the evenings, and instead sat and watched TV with her mom until she indicated she was ready for bed. It was early, but Lisa tucked into her own bed after taking care of her mom. This was a different kind of tired than she was used to. One where her body was done for the day, but her thoughts seemed to be just getting started. She didn't know how to cope with this new life she suddenly was in. Someone else was relying on her for everything, her expenses had more than doubled, and she couldn't care less about her freelance clients. With no solutions presenting themselves, she finally dozed off.

The rest of the summer passed in a haze. Lisa struggled to keep up with the demands of her job, her freelance work, her mom, and her apartment. Most of the time she felt like she was barely coping. Now, instead of having time to wander the park in the sun on a Sunday afternoon, she was trying to clean the house, get groceries, plan meals, and get her mom's personal needs taken care of.

The change in scenery that Lisa thought would improve her mom's health actually seemed to make it worse. Sometimes she wasn't able to get up before Lisa left work in the morning, and she'd have to take the bus home on an extended lunch hour to help her mom get up and have something to eat before getting back on the bus to head back to work. She drove the car in a few times, but the time she spent trying to find affordable parking downtown cut too much into her workday.

Her bosses had been understanding so far, but after having someone totally committed to her job, they were beginning to question Lisa's ability to handle everything. She took advantage of the workplace counseling service again, and it helped to know her concerns were valid, and quite normal considering the circumstances. They suggested she find a caregiver's support group where she could talk with others who were caring for family members, but Lisa couldn't see how to fit that into her schedule.

In September things escalated unexpectedly. Lisa made a trip home at lunch again to help her mom get up, but her mom wouldn't budge. She was paler than usual and begged Lisa to just leave her there. Desperate, Lisa called the toll free healthcare line, and they advised her to have her mom brought to the emergency department. After talking with them she got her mom up, and then it was like her legs just gave out from under her and Lisa could only try to cushion her mom's fall. With her free hand, she reached her cell phone in her blazer pocket and called 911.

It wasn't until ten that night when Lisa was called into a consultation room to speak with a doctor. They did well at getting her mom a semi-private bed in the Emergency Department and getting her hooked up to an IV, but then there was a series of tests and waiting for results.

The kind-looking doctor smiled and asked how she was before proceeding. But as he asked her some simple questions, she found she didn't have much to offer. She didn't know when her mom had last seen her family doctor, she didn't know if she was on any medications except aspirin for the pain, and she could only guess at who her mom's former doctor was, since she couldn't even remember the name of the health clinic in her hometown.

Tears pooled in her eyes as she apologized to the doctor, "I only saw my mom for the first time in four years this summer after my dad died. Before that I had only talked to her once a year on her birthday. I didn't even know she had arthritis until the day of the funeral when she needed my help getting dressed. I've been trying to take care of her, but it's so hard to do that and still earn enough money to cover everything. I'll try to do better, but I need to know how to fix this!"

"Hey," the doctor leaned forward and looked at her "This is *not* your fault! It's a big challenge to suddenly be a caregiver, and every time I've checked on your mom today she's told me how good you are to her. It's clear that she has health challenges that need to be addressed, but we can do that and help her feel better, OK?"

Lisa nodded and tried to smile, but she still felt guilty. She had planned on getting her mom to the doctor after they moved, but she hadn't wanted to take time off work to take her in and so she put it off. That needed to change, and she had to figure out a way to take better care of her mom and still keep her job.

The hospital discharged her mom just after midnight, with instructions to follow up with a doctor the next day when the rest of the test results were in. The emergency room doctor would take them on as temporary patients, but Lisa would have to register her mom with a full-time family doctor as soon as possible.

She dragged herself to work the next morning before leaving early again so she could take her mom to the doctor. When they got in to see him, he had more life-changing information.

"Mrs. Naylor, are you aware that you have rheumatoid arthritis?"

"Well, I'm not sure… Robert took me to the doctor a while ago when I couldn't get out of bed by myself anymore. The doctor said it was arthritis and I should see a specialist, but Robert insisted that I would be fine." Lisa felt her stomach start to churn at the realization that her dad had prevented her mom from getting proper care.

"How have you been managing the pain?"

"Oh, well, I take a few aspirin every morning, and then whatever I need throughout the day."

The doctor frowned, "Have you been having any stomach pains?"

"Yes, all the time doctor! How did you know?"

"The amount of aspirin you're taking is very hard on your stomach. It looks like you've had some internal bleeding from it. That, along with the inflammation from the rheumatoid arthritis caused anemia, which is why you didn't have enough energy to get out of bed yesterday. It's not often that things get this serious, but without the proper care things can go wrong quickly. Now, I'm not a specialist, but I'll adjust the medicines you're taking, and we'll try to get your symptoms under control until you can get in to see a rheumatologist."

The doctor prescribed a pain killer that would give Maria more relief from the pain, along with an antacid that would help to ease some of the stomach irritation that came from the medication. He also suggested she take care to eat a healthy balanced diet, and consider taking a fish oil supplement every day.

They left with a handful of prescriptions to fill and Lisa feeling nearly overwhelmed with grief and guilt. She took her mom back home and got her settled in an armchair with a cup of tea before heading back out to get the prescriptions filled. The pharmacist was very understanding when she realized that Lisa was trying to understand her mom's illness for the first time. She brought her into a consultation room where she took time to answer Lisa's questions, and give her a better understanding of what her mom was going through.

It seemed terribly unfair to Lisa that her mom's own body was attacking her joints and taking away any chance of a quality life just when she got free of an abusive husband. The old house had sold for more than any of them expected, and Lisa was thrilled that her mom had a healthy bank account and all her debts were paid in full. But how could she enjoy any sort of life if she couldn't even get out of bed in the morning?

The pharmacist assured her that rheumatoid arthritis was generally a manageable condition and with the right care they could expect the disease to go into remission for undetermined amounts of time. But Lisa wasn't very optimistic. It felt like a life sentence to her, and she was left with trying to explain it to her mom without getting too negative about her future.

When she got home, she sat for a few minutes in the car trying to compose herself before going in. Realizing she was too tired to cook dinner, she started the car and went to buy takeout again.

Over dinner, she tried to explain to her mom the diagnosis, and how they could help her feel better. She conveyed more optimism than she was actually feeling, and her mom went to bed thinking that she would be better soon. Lisa could only hope she was right.

After cleaning up supper Lisa made a fresh cup of coffee and got to work. There wasn't much she could do for her day job remotely, but she could make sure all her freelance jobs were caught up to date. Even though she wasn't sure how to fit it in, she also let each of them know that she was taking on more clients. She needed to increase her income to keep up with the additional expenses she was facing.

The next morning Lisa felt like a bus had driven over her, but her mom was ready to get up and have breakfast! On the pharmacist's advice, she woke her up early to take a pain pill and let it take effect before trying to get up. It certainly made the morning routine go easier, and Lisa felt confident leaving her mom when she went to work. She explained that she needed to work late for a few days to get caught up, and her mom assured her she'd call if she couldn't handle the long day away from Lisa's help. Lisa was torn between hoping her mom didn't need her, and hoping she'd actually call if she did need her.

During a short coffee break at lunchtime, Lisa called Janet. They had texted a bit back and forth since her dad had died but hadn't actually talked. Lisa needed her wise and level-headed friend to help her get a grip on her new life. Janet was extremely understanding and could relate to exactly how Lisa was feeling, since it was similar to what she was going through with her own dad. The only difference was that she was in a financial position to delegate more of her work so she could take the time to care for her dad and get him to all of his appointments without giving up work commitments.

She suggested that Lisa register as a caregiver with the government and talk to HR at Golden Lion about changing her level of taxation on her paychecks to reflect this. There were some tax breaks offered for people caring for loved ones that could ease Lisa's burden a little bit. After getting off the phone Lisa added it to her growing 'To Do' list and turned back to her work.

For the rest of the week Lisa didn't get home until after eight as she worked to catch up and prove to her employers that she could still handle all the responsibility of her position. After a short visit with her mom and helping her into bed, she'd return to the kitchen table with a cup of coffee and work some more.

CHAPTER 27

Slowly Lisa got used to her new schedule and felt a little less overwhelmed. Two new clients came in as referrals, but after reviewing their situations, she only took on one of them. While she would love the challenge that the second one offered, she knew she couldn't give them the level of service they'd need to get their books in order. By her calculations, she needed to put in an extra twenty hours a week to keep up with her freelance work. As long as she put in two hours every weekday evening and a full day on Saturday, she'd manage but she realized she couldn't keep doing it forever.

It wasn't until the end of October that they could see a rheumatologist for the first time. Since her office was at the other end of the city Lisa booked off the day from work so she wouldn't feel pressured for time. It was a nice change to enjoy a leisurely morning with her mom before leaving for their eleven o'clock appointment. Dr. Gabe was a young-looking, energetic, and enthusiastic lady. Her curly blonde hair practically exploded from her ponytail, and she bounced on her toes whenever she wasn't examining Maria. Lisa guessed that she wore through at least a few pairs of sneakers every year!

She confirmed the diagnosis of rheumatoid arthritis or RA as she called it for short, and gave the same optimistic outlook that the pharmacist gave. Most patients who followed her instructions could look forward to times in remission when they experienced barely any symptoms, and when they had 'flares' they could get in to see her quickly, now that Maria was registered with her.

Although the new medication made a big difference in Maria's ability to get up in the mornings and make it through her day without too much pain, Dr. Gabe felt they could better manage the symptoms with a different prescription. She also suggested Maria find an RA exercise group or join a gym that offered low impact exercise classes, and that they both switch to a diet that contained more whole foods and less processed foods.

When they were ready to leave, she asked for their family doctor's name and address so she could pass on the medical information. Lisa admitted that she still hadn't found one. Dr. Gabe asked her to prioritize it so that they could be supported by a full medical team.

Lisa's mom suggested they eat lunch out, and she would treat. Although she just wanted to go home and hide in bed, Lisa agreed. Eating out helped to perk her up, and they took a short walk to the medical supply store nearby. It was another thing she had meant to do for quite a while. When they walked out Lisa felt better. They already had a shower chair to put in the bathtub, but now she also had a grab bar that she could install herself and take when they left. Plus, they had fitted her mom with a walker she could use on days when her legs were stiff, which would take some of the physical pressure off Lisa.

However, the best resource they came away with was the name of a mobility expert that Lisa could hire when she bought a house who would assess the place and help them make the best choices for making it accessible.

Sandra, the mortgage broker had been incredibly patient with Lisa for the last few months. She assured her that her credit was continuing to improve, and even though Lisa hadn't been able to put much more into savings for a house, she had caught up from the extra expenses of the summer and her dad's funeral and cremation without getting into debt. When she was ready to look, Sandra would proceed with her mortgage preapproval, but she suggested that Lisa could consider any reasonable houses up to $380,000. The thought of committing to spending that much money was frightening. Her mom offered to contribute to the down payment, but Lisa wasn't comfortable with that option either.

She found a family doctor accepting new patients and made an intake appointment for both her and her mom. Although she hadn't seen a doctor in at least ten years, she decided it wouldn't hurt to have one just in case. But the day of their appointment in early November Maria woke up with the flu and they had to cancel. Lisa couldn't imagine where her mom had gotten it, since she barely went out, but she could sympathize.

Worried about leaving her mom home alone during the day, Lisa called Amy—her former roommate and experienced care aide. Amy still lived with her aunt and worked occasionally at the care home, but she had the day free and was at Lisa's place before ten that morning. Lisa was more than happy to pay Amy's day rate in exchange for knowing her mom would be ok.

It took a week for Maria to recover from the flu, and it was credit to Amy's daytime care and Lisa's nighttime care that she was on the mend so soon. Amy explained to Lisa that the medication Maria took to control her RA also suppressed her immune system so she was more likely to get sick and take longer to recover. Lisa knew they had been told something about that when they saw Dr. Gabe, but she had forgotten. She'd have to be far more careful about who she was around at work, and to wash her hands right away whenever she came home. It seemed likely that she had brought the virus home, and she didn't want it to happen again.

By the time they could get back in for their intake appointments it was the beginning of December. This time everyone stayed healthy, and they met their new family doctor. He was nice enough, but obviously in a rush, and wanting to get the appointment over quickly.

However, he told them they could see the Physician's Assistant, Kara Wilson, at the clinic for most concerns and would have a shorter wait for an appointment. Lisa booked an appointment for a week later.

For the first time, Lisa would take time off over Christmas. In the past, Christmas was a time to keep busy and not think about family. But this year was special because she could enjoy the time with her mom. She booked off a week beginning on the 20th and was already working to make sure other people in her department could cover for her when she was away. There was no way she would take time off, just to come back to double the workload because nothing had gotten done without her! She learned that lesson after her dad's death.

The company bosses were back to being completely happy with Lisa and her work and she breathed a sigh of relief that she could still count on keeping that position. She received an end-of-year bonus of $7,000 after taxes which was an exciting boost to her savings. As one of the new senior level employees, she hadn't known what type of bonus to expect. Lisa was proud that she would close out the year with over $94,000 in her savings. She hoped that the next year would be the one when she could buy her first home.

Changes in the weather over the next week really slowed Maria down, and it was the first thing Lisa brought up with Kara, the Physician's Assistant, when she met with her . She had to look up the term before coming because she didn't know what a Physician's Assistant was. Basically, she was an extension of the family doctor, and able to take care of many health needs. Lisa took one look at Kara and decided she liked her. She was average height, a little bit curvy, with shoulder length brown hair and a smile that lit up her entire face. Everything about Kara said she was happy and approachable — even her lab coat that was covered in little rainbows!

Lisa planned on asking Kara if she could get a wheelchair for her mom and leaving it at that. But she found herself confiding in her about the challenges she was facing in her new life as a caregiver and how hard it was to always be responsible for her mom. Kara listened quietly the entire time. She assured Lisa that everything she was going through was as normal as something so life-changing could be. Then she took out a notepad (with rainbows!) and wrote down a name and a phone number.

"This is my friend Carrie. Her mom was in a bad car accident when she was ten years old, and she helped take care of her until she left for university. I want you to call and talk to her. It's one thing to tell me everything, and I sympathize greatly and will try to help, but Carrie will listen and relate in a different way. Plus she's been through a lot of major challenges in her life, just like you. Us women need to support each other. Promise you'll call her?"

Lisa couldn't say no to Kara, and she promised she'd call, even though she didn't think it would help. Before she left, Kara gave her the name of a wheelchair supply company that gave the best prices available. "You'll want to save your resources wherever possible, so this will help. Keep the receipt, you can claim it as a medical expense. And please call me if anything comes up, no matter how small. You're not alone in this, we all want to help you and your mom enjoy your new life together."

As she left, Lisa had to agree with Dr. Gabe's assessment that it helped to have a whole team on board with her mom's care. Knowing she had people to call really did take a little pressure off her. She stopped and picked up a wheelchair for her mom. After a brief 'driving' lesson she struggled to collapse it to put into the trunk of the car until another customer came and showed her a few tricks. He laughingly told her she'd be a pro in no time. He turned out to be right.

CHAPTER 28

Lisa took the first day of her Christmas holidays to do nothing but relax and help her mom. She had worked long hours for the past few weeks at work, with her freelance clients, and even doing some Christmas preparations so she could really and truly take this time off.

In the afternoon they went out to buy a little Christmas tree and ornaments. Past Christmases had been decidedly disappointing for both women—although neither knew the other's feelings at the time. There hadn't even been any ornaments worth keeping from the old house. This year they would start new, happy traditions.

Lisa also bought tickets for them both to see the Nutcracker—something she had always wanted to do. And of course, there would be Boxing Day celebrations at Manuel and Betsy's. Betsy came over about once a month, and her visits were something Maria always looked forward to. Lisa was pleased that her mom was starting to have things to look forward to. Maria tried to hint to Lisa that grandchildren would be the best gift she could get, but Lisa laughingly told her she'd need more children first before she had a chance for grandchildren!

The day before they went to see the Nutcracker, Lisa and Maria did something they had never enjoyed together before—shopping for outfits. When Lisa was a child, her dad always insisted on shopping with them, and only if it was things they absolutely needed. Now, free to look at anything they wanted, and with their own bank accounts that they were in control of, they could enjoy shopping, even surrounded by all the stressed out Christmas shoppers. Navigating crowds in a wheelchair was also a new experience, as Lisa figured out how to push the wheelchair without running over anyone's toes or bumping into corners!

For Maria, shopping without being told what to buy was liberating *and* challenging. It had been decades since she had thought about what *she* wanted, and for over an hour they wandered in and out of stores without any clear direction. Finally, Lisa stopped at a bench with a free space and sat down. "Mom, just look at the women as they go by, and tell me when you see a look you like. We won't find anything if you don't know what you're looking for!" Lisa thought back to the stylist she had almost hired when she needed her own new look. If it came to that she'd happily pay the cost if only to get her mom out of the worn out blouses and polyester slacks that comprised her entire wardrobe.

While her mom watched the shoppers, Lisa watched her mom. She wore her thin brown hair straight down her back, often pulled into a braid. Lisa knew she had been born shortly after her parents got married, but she always thought of her mom as old. She wasn't, really. She wondered if her mom had ever had her hair done properly, or worn make-up, or even felt beautiful. The past six months had been entirely focused on practicalities—keeping her job and her freelance clients, getting groceries and cleaning the house, and now trying to find the right medical help for her mom. Things like how her mom *felt* had completely escaped her thoughts until now.

Leaning her arm on the wheelchair, Lisa asked, "Mom, how do you feel right now?"

Her mom turned to her, surprised. "Truly Lisa, I feel happier than

I've ever felt before. I feel like maybe my life has a chance at something...although I don't know what that something is. And I feel so grateful to be with you. It's like a brand new life, really."

"You know... you're still young. Way too young to be dressing like that! I think we've been going in the wrong stores. Do you see anyone wearing anything you like?"

"See that lady over there with the leggings and the purple top and the scarf? I like that, and I think it would be comfortable too. I always liked the idea of fitted jeans with a nice pair of boots, but I'm afraid denim would be too painful for me with the arthritis."

"Excellent! Let's go find that outfit, and maybe some cute boots to go with it!"

With a style in mind, Lisa pointed the wheelchair towards a completely different set of stores. Even though they were busy, salespeople were happy to help them once Marie described what she was looking for. It took a while to try things on, especially when they had to wait for the accessible changerooms, but it was worth it.

By the afternoon, Maria was the proud owner of a new little wardrobe. With her own money, she bought leggings in black, navy, and mustard, some tunics in colors that matched all the leggings, two colorful scarves, a casual blazer that could be worn as a jacket or to dress up an outfit, black slip-on ankle boots, and a pretty navy blue wrap dress that had a ruffle around the collar that brought out her flawless light skin. Just as they were about to leave, Lisa veered into a shoe store where they found a pair of silver flats to wear with the dress, or with leggings when the weather warmed up.

At her mom's insistence, Lisa tried on a deep red dress that had a fitted bodice with a short, flared skirt. It was very 1950s and something Lisa would have never tried on her own, but once she had it on, she fell in love with it. They would hit the town in style tomorrow night!

Once they were home, it was obvious the day had taken a lot out of Maria, and Lisa helped her in bed for a rest before starting supper.

She had really splurged for Christmas and bought her mom a special recliner that was ergonomically designed for a smaller frame, and motorized so her mom could lay all the way back, or slowly bring herself to a standing position. It was getting delivered on the 24th, and Lisa hoped it would help her mom spend her days in more comfort and be able to rest during the daytime without having to go to bed.

With time to spare she finally called the number the physician's assistant Kara gave to her weeks before. Even over the phone, Lisa felt an instant connection with Carrie. It was as if she only needed a few short sentences to understand exactly how Lisa was feeling about suddenly being completely responsible for her mom, and she made it sound like the things Lisa was going through were understandable.

They talked a bit, and then Carrie surprised Lisa by asking if she'd like to meet up in person. She had thought this was just a one-time phone call, but she loved the idea of talking to Carrie again. They agreed to meet in the new year at Carrie's house.

Christmas Day was perfect. Maria was delighted with her new chair, and after a few tries she was able to get up and down without any help. Lisa breathed a sigh of relief to know her mom would have a bit more independence on the days when she was at work and her mom was in pain. The good days and bad days were impossible to predict, so anything that alleviated some challenges was a good thing.

For Christmas dinner, Lisa took her mom to the restaurant she used to work at every Christmas Day. A few people she recognized were still working there and it was nice to introduce her mom to some of the people she spent so much time with in the past. They ended the day drinking mulled wine that Lisa had received as a gift from work, and watching Christmas movies.

As usual, Boxing Day at Manuel and Betsy's was loud, fun, and packed with delicious food. Lisa brought the wheelchair along just in case, but Maria was having a good day, and made it up the outside steps to the main level where she was immediately surrounded by Betsy and her aunts. In a patchwork patterned tunic with an orange scarf and the mustard colored leggings, her style matched the happiness and outgoing personality that her face already radiated.

Lisa was amazed at her mom's transformation. She had never had the chance to watch her with other people and hadn't realized how much of a people person her mom really was. Lisa was much happier to sit on the sidelines and watch everything around her, but she was discovering that her mom preferred being right in the middle of everything. If only there was a way she could do something during the weekdays. She thought back to her mom's dream to be a preschool teacher. With her RA that might not be possible. She wished they could find *something* her mom could do!

CHAPTER 29

Lisa entered the new year determined that this year she would buy her first home. Her focus had changed from her old goal of simply owning a house that could generate a lot of income. Now, her home would be a place she could set up long term for her mom's needs while still working towards her own financial goals, and she decided she had waited and saved long enough.

Besides, now that she was coping well with the demands of work, freelancing, and her mom, she wanted the next challenge!

When she visited Carrie again, it only renewed her resolve. From the little bit she knew about her (since Carrie kept most of the conversation about Lisa), Carrie was putting herself through university while raising two kids and working on her own business making really cool picture frames. Lisa knew her mom would love the brightly colored frames—another reason to buy her own house so she could put up whatever she wanted on the walls!

One thing Carrie mentioned again was the importance of Lisa getting help for her mom. At first Lisa thought she was handling everything just fine. But as they talked, she admitted that helping her mom shower was still uncomfortable for both of them and something she'd rather not do. On the back of that thought came the realization that Amy may be the perfect solution. Maria had felt completely comfortable with Amy when she was sick with the flu, and Lisa suspected she would also prefer to not have her own daughter helping with some of her more personal care needs.

Before she drove away from Carrie's she called Amy and asked if she might hire her. Amy was delighted with the chance to help Lisa out and give her a break. Not only did she already understand what it was like to care for someone full-time, she had the training and skills to take good care of Maria and make sure she was safe. It was the perfect solution, and when Lisa got home and talked to Maria about it, she agreed. She also insisted on paying Amy out of her own savings, which took another little worry off Lisa's shoulders.

That Saturday they went out again to meet Carrie and her kids at an indoor kids' play place—another of Carrie's suggestions. As soon as they were in the door Carrie walked over and introduced Matthew and Katie to them before the two kids ran off to play. Matthew was polite and sincere as he reached his hand out to each of them as he said hello. Katie, already jumping on her toes in anticipation of going to play barely got out an excited "I LOVE your scarf!" to Maria before Carrie let them go.

Laughing, the three of them stopped at the little café area to buy drinks before settling at a table facing the play area. They both thanked Carrie for suggesting bringing in help for Maria's care, and talked about how much it was helping already. Carrie asked some questions about RA and what their day-to-day lives were like.

Soon Maria was sharing more with Carrie about her past than Lisa had known.

"I knew soon after marrying Robert that I had made a big mistake. But back then you were just expected to make the best of your marriage—even if it was bad. The first time I really wanted to leave was when Lisa was about ten years old. We used to get along so well when he was working. But then one day when he was home she said she wished he was always at work so she could spend every day with me.

He got so mad at me about that. He said if I ever tried to turn her against him again he'd take her away and I'd never see her again. After that I was so afraid of losing her, I tried to keep my distance from her so he wouldn't think I was trying to turn her away from him.

When Lisa moved out, I was so terribly lonely. I started to put aside any change I found in his pockets when I did laundry, and sometimes I'd walk to the stores during the day to return things for a little bit of cash. I had enough saved for a bus ride to the city when he found the money I had hidden away. It was terrible… and then the arthritis started. The happiest day of my life was when Lisa said she wanted me to move in with her!"

Lisa sat there reeling from this new information while the noise of happy children playing swirled around her head. Her mom had *wanted* to leave and was going to come find her? And the whole time she had seemed so withdrawn when Lisa was growing up her mom was *protecting* her? She struggled to turn her focus back to the conversation where Carrie was asking her mom what she wanted to do now.

Maria seemed surprised by the question and sat drinking her coffee for a minute before answering. "I'm just not used to thinking about things like that. Robert was in charge of everything, and I did what he told me because that was what I felt I had to do. I've wanted to get a job for a long time, but I don't know if there's anything left that I can do. I need to sit, and I can't do anything that requires much strength. I never went to college or anything…"

"What do you like doing?"

Lisa watched her mom struggle to answer the question. Carrie put a hand on Maria's arm, "Maria, you did what you had to do to survive during your marriage. I did the same thing. But now you get to have a new start. The thing is, you'll need to practice a new way of thinking. I can tell that Lisa accepts you just where you are, so you don't need to worry about pleasing her. This is a wonderful opportunity you have! So, what do you like?"

Maria smiled. "I like this. I like talking to people and having conversations. I like looking around and seeing happy children playing. I've been so lonely. I want to be around people now!"

They spent time talking about different jobs Maria might be suited for. Lisa loved the way Carrie could shift their focus, so they were thinking about the future and not trying to work through all the things in the past. It was true, even though Maria had lived through many terrible years, the only thing she had power over was what she did next. Lisa wanted to help her create a good, fulfilling life—whatever that looked like.

CHAPTER 30

By the end of January Lisa was the proud owner of a mortgage pre-approval. Sandra had worked incredibly hard on her behalf, and Lisa couldn't wait to start house shopping. The pre-approval was for up to $395,000 but Lisa was hoping to find something under $350,000 and put 25% down. That would give her a good head start paying off the mortgage, while still having cash for renovations.

February kicked off with an unexpected snowstorm and Lisa's plans (along with everyone else's in the city) ground to a halt. Instead of meeting in person with the real estate agent Sandra had recommended and then going to see houses on the weekend, Lisa was stuck with a brief phone call to review what she was looking for, and then nothing. She caught up on all her freelance work, cleaned their little apartment and then sat waiting for the roads to clear. It wasn't until Wednesday that she could get back into work, and she worked long days for the rest of the week to catch up.

Saturday morning the real estate agent was at their apartment by ten for Lisa's first proper venture into house hunting. They agreed that Maria would stay home and only go with Lisa if she found places she wanted to see a second time. Between the slippery sidewalks and her walking challenges it just wasn't worth the risk and time for her to come along.

The agent seemed nice. He was an older gentleman who had gotten his real estate license after retiring because he didn't like staying home as much as he thought he would! He introduced himself when Lisa opened the door, "Hello, I'm Frank Wright."

She shook his hand and brought him in to meet her mom before they left again. Frank had set up appointments to see four houses. They ranged in price from $327,000 to $415,000. Lisa raised her eyebrows at the last number, but he assured her that it had been on the market for quite some time, and the price was negotiable.

Her checklist of features felt vague, but Frank said she'd find it easier to clarify what she wanted when she was actually walking through houses. To start she was looking for:

- under her budget of $395,000
- first floor that was, or could be made wheelchair accessible
- near the city center or a good bus route
- at least four bedrooms

The first house they looked at had five steps to the front door. Frank assured Lisa she could have a ramp built, but she had trouble picturing it. Inside the house seemed nice, but there were two steps up into the kitchen on the main floor, and then another two steps down into the living room. He apologized, as the interior steps hadn't been in the description, and they left.

The rest of the houses they looked at wouldn't work for one reason or another. Lisa tried to look for the potential in the least expensive house but the layout inside was so awkward she couldn't see how it could be made into a workable space for anyone, let alone someone with a wheelchair.

She felt discouraged, but Frank wasn't deterred. "You're in a perfect position to find the right place, Lisa. You're not under pressure because your own house just sold or anything like that, and you aren't limited to one school district or neighborhood. I'll look at everything out there, and we *will* find your future home and it'll be worth all the time we've spent looking."

He promised to be in touch throughout the week and would take Lisa through houses again the next weekend. After he left, she made a cup of coffee and had a chat with her mom about the different houses before moving to the table and getting to work on her free-lance jobs. The shift in focus helped, and by the time she put everything away to start supper she felt better. There was nothing she could do to make the right house come any sooner, and Frank was right, it would be worth it to wait for the right one.

The other big challenge on her mind was her mom's situation. She could see her starting to fade a little after the fun and socializing they had done over Christmas. Her mom needed to be out and with people. It suddenly occurred to Lisa that a new look might help too. Over supper of chicken alfredo and green salad, she asked if her mom wanted to go to her hairdresser. Maria often commented on how much she loved Lisa's 'new' hairdo. She reached back and ran her hand down her braid before answering, "I don't know, I've had my hair like this since you were born…I guess that's a pretty good reason to have a change!"

Lisa promised to make an appointment with Sheila. She continued to go back to the lady who had helped her create her own new style and Sheila followed Lisa's personal journey with great pride. The other workers at the salon often talked about Lisa's transformation from wallflower to business tycoon. She always laughed and told them she wasn't *that* important at work, but it made her feel good to know what they thought of her.

Sheila was booked on the weekends for the next month, so Lisa arranged for Amy to take Maria in for a haircut and style during the week. It was a perfect early birthday gift. Having Amy available was a godsend. Lisa didn't know how she had handled everything on her own before having help.

For Amy, the break from caring for her aunt was welcome. The past few months Aunt Helena had slowed down and now spent most of her time in bed. Although Amy was used to caring for people at the care home in the same situation, it was different when it was family and it helped to have a change of scenery.

The day of Maria's haircut, Amy called Lisa at work. "Lisa? Sorry to bother you at work, but I'd like to bring your mom over to the office to show off her new haircut and then I think we should go out for lunch together!"

Lisa had a lot to do at work, but she agreed. She had wanted to bring her mom to the office for quite a while, but it was tricky to plan when she couldn't get there on her own. This would be a nice opportunity to show her where she worked, and she'd try to keep lunch short so she could get back to work.

When Sarah brought Amy and her mom around the corner to Lisa's desk, Lisa was speechless. Her plain-looking mom was transformed into a bright, stylish, and much younger version of herself! Not only had Sheila given her a stunning haircut, she added highlights that were amazing. Her hair was short and stacked in the back, with slightly longer layers in the front that swept across her forehead. The dark blonde highlights seemed to make her eyes sparkle, and the cut brought out the soft lines in her heart-shaped face.

"Mom! You look... I can't even say... just so so wonderful!" Lisa reached down and hugged her mom. She smelled like a bouquet of wildflowers from the shampoo Sheila used.

"I know, isn't it a great cut?" Amy looked nearly as happy as Maria with the outcome. "I made an appointment to see Sheila too, she's fantastic!"

"Here, let me get my purse and jacket and I'll show you around before we grab lunch." Lisa was so proud to introduce her mom to her co-workers. None of them knew her whole story, and they just thought it was nice that Lisa got along so well with her mom now that she had to live with her.

She took them around the corner to a cute little restaurant she had been to once before. Her tradition of buying something cheap for lunch on the way to work changed now that she had her own kitchen, and she usually brought a sandwich and a piece of fruit to eat at her desk. She had to admit, it was nice to get out of the office in the middle of the day.

CHAPTER 31

J ust as they were finishing their meals, Lisa's phone rang.
Looking at the name, she wondered why Frank was calling in
the middle of the week. They went out every Saturday in
February with no success in finding anything right for Lisa's situation. She apologized to the others before answering.

"Lisa? Listen, I'm sorry to bother you during the workday, but I
think I might have found your house. Another agent at our office
here has just signed a listing. It's got a level entrance, a big office on
the main floor that you could easily convert to a bedroom, four
bedrooms up, and a walk-out basement you can develop."

"That sounds great! Can we take a look on Saturday then?"

"Well, that's the thing. The sellers are in a tight situation, and they
need to sell immediately. It's priced below market value and I think it
will be gone before the weekend. If you're interested you need to
move on it. It'll be up on the main website tonight at seven but the
agent has agreed to let us in now if you can make it."

Lisa took a big breath. This might be the chance she had been
dreaming of. "Alright, let's make it happen. If you give me the

address I can take a taxi over and meet you there right away." She clarified the details with him and hung up before looking at the two beaming women at the table with her.

"Frank's found a house. Maybe *the* house, but I need to go right away if I want it. So I'll leave you two here to enjoy the rest of your lunch and hopefully I'll have good news!"

"Oh, this is so exciting!" Maria would have jumped up and down if she could, but instead she clapped her hands together before reaching out to give Lisa a hug. Quickly Lisa pulled some cash out of her wallet to pay for the lunch and then dashed outside to grab a taxi.

As she was riding to the house, she called Sarah to let her know she'd be late, and then she tried to compose herself. She realized she hadn't even asked Frank what the price of the house was, but she was confident he wouldn't take her somewhere that was out of her budget.

It was a good thing Frank was standing on the sidewalk when the taxi pulled up, or Lisa wouldn't have even noticed the house. Set back from the road and hidden by overgrown shrubs, there was nothing attractive about the front of the house. Paint was peeling from the siding, and the garage door was open about six inches and looked broken.

"So, this is my dream home, huh?" She teased him.

"Granted, it's not much to look at on the outside. Let's go inside."

They walked towards the front door. What might have been a front porch had a weather-worn recliner, some trash, and a pile of plant pots with dead plants in them. Frank took a key out of his pocket and let them in.

The front entryway was a good size, with a door to the right, stairs just past the door leading up, and a large living room to the left. Dark paint gave a gloomy feeling to the whole area, but Lisa could already see that this house had more space than any other they had seen.

"Here, this must be the office you can convert to a bedroom." Henry opened the door to the right and they walked into a large room with more dark paint, but a big window facing the front porch. They followed the room to a second door which led past a full bathroom and into the kitchen at the back of the house.

It looked like the current owners had started renovations here. While the cupboards and countertops looked new, the appliances were dated and the floor was older linoleum. Lisa liked the dark lower cupboards and the contrast of the white upper cabinets. She recognized granite on the countertops although she still wasn't sure why everyone made such a bit deal about it.

To the right was a door leading into a utility room with a disgusting looking washer and dryer, and then into the single garage which was piled so full of stuff that no light could seep in from the broken garage door. Frank told her that the house would be sold 'as is' with the new owner responsible for clearing out everything remaining in the house. The current owners had taken what they wanted and would not be returning to the house.

Back into the kitchen (which was quickly becoming the nicest room in the house) Lisa noticed that there was a big window above the large sink, and the counter had room for barstools on the other side of it. Sliding doors led out from the dining area onto a deck that looked over a very overgrown back yard.

From the large living room with windows facing the side of the house and the front yard, they went back through the entryway up the stairs to the second floor. Every room was a different, disturbing color and the carpet was stained and worn, but the layout was good. The master bedroom was a nice size with a walk-in closet, a sitting area, and a full bathroom.

The other three bedrooms all had big windows but were in desperate need of paint and new flooring. Two of the bedrooms shared a Jack and Jill bathroom, leaving Lisa and Frank to wonder what the person in the last bedroom did for a bathroom. Either they went through the other bedroom, or they used the downstairs bathroom. It was a bit weird!

Lisa was already feeling like she could make this house work—although it would be a lot of work and money—before Frank reminded her they still needed to see the basement. The door to the basement was just past the stairs by the front entrance.

When they turned the corner at the bottom of the basement stairs, they both let out a "Wow!" Someone had let loose with spray paint—a lot of spray paint. Every surface was covered in very amateur graffiti. The unfinished ceiling, the walls covered in plastic vapor barrier, and the cement floor were a kaleidoscope of neon swirls. It was almost impossible to look beyond the painting disaster, but there was definitely potential. Big windows and a sliding door faced out into the yard, and might let in a decent amount of sunlight if they weren't painted over. To the right was an exterior door and another interior door. Looking inside there was a full bathroom that had mercifully been spared an attack of spray paint.

Frank looked around the expanse of color, "With a bathroom already here, you could put up a little kitchenette and rent this out as a separate space, easily with two bedrooms. I'd have to check the zoning, but it's possible it's already zoned for a secondary suite. If that's the case, you can probably get $1,200 for this, plus the rooms upstairs that you can rent out."

He walked over to another door near the stairs that they had missed in the crazy décor. Inside was a large furnace room with a newer looking hot water tank. Along one side were industrial shelves.

They went back upstairs, and Lisa had to admit the upstairs looked much nicer once it was compared with the basement. "Alright Frank. I admit, this could be the right house for me. Let me brace myself while you tell me the price."

He smiled, "I've been waiting for this! Now, keep in mind that there's a lot of work needed, and the sale will be 'as is' so even if an inspection shows up something major, they won't negotiate further. They're asking $312,000."

"What? No way! Seriously?"

"Absolutely. They want to sell right away, with immediate possession. If you want the place, I suggest you make an offer of $315,000 and give a $10,000 cash deposit. We're the first ones in, so that's good, but I know that investors will look past the cosmetic problems in the house and see the potential. It will be sold by the end of the week. The only question is if you want to be the buyer or not."

Lisa walked around the main floor again. There was a huge risk in buying something like this. But she thought the opportunity outweighed the risk. Between the accessibility, the set-up with rooms and bathrooms, and the potential in the basement, this house could definitely become her dream house *and* a great investment. She walked back to the entryway where Frank was waiting for her.

"Let's do it! I want to put in an offer right away with the terms you've suggested."

He reached out and shook her hand, "Congratulations! Let's go back to my office and finalize the paperwork."

While he drove Lisa called Sandra to make sure everything was in order with her mortgage to make the offer. Sandra said she would fax the paperwork to Henry's office so they could prove that Lisa was prepared to purchase the house immediately.

Frank brought Lisa into a small conference room and introduced her to the seller's agent Jennifer Munroe. "It's not common for us to all be in the same room during negotiations, but this is a special case."

While Lisa and Frank waited, Jennifer called her client to present them the offer. Two minutes later everyone was shaking Lisa's hand again and congratulating her. "That's it? It's mine?"

After years of dreaming, scrimping, and saving, and weeks of looking at houses that were never quite right, Lisa could hardly believe it was all suddenly finished.

"Well, we do still have some paperwork to sign. The owners aren't in town, so we'll sign all the paperwork here, and overnight it to the owners. Once they've signed everything they'll send us the documents electronically. I've dealt with your mortgage broker before, and Sandra's fantastic. She'll make sure everything moves quickly. I expect to give you the keys to your new home in a few days." Jennifer smiled at Lisa. "It's a lot to take in, but I think you're going to be really happy with that house once you've fixed it up. I would have jumped on it myself, but my teenagers would kill me if I made them move. This kind of deal only comes around once in a lifetime." She looked up at Frank, "And now you owe me a bottle of wine!"

Frank laughed, "Done! Thanks for holding off until I got Lisa to see the place." He turned to Lisa, "She gave me two hours before she started calling buyers. You just made it in time!"

He offered to drive her back to work, and she agreed. Frank was a good man, and smart enough to leave her to her thoughts on the twenty minute drive back to her office. She had done it. She had her first home! There were so many thoughts and feelings spinning through her head she couldn't settle on just one.

Finally she could give her mom a safe and permanent place to live. And she could really put down roots. She could do whatever she wanted to the house because it was *hers*! All of the years of saving, of working two jobs, of not going on vacation or buying a car or going out for dinner—it all seemed like such a small price to pay now. This was it!

Her old focus on getting rich was nothing compared to the feeling of security and confidence that buying the house gave her. Sure, she'd be worth a lot more next year because she had bought this house. But that hardly mattered. The biggest thing was having a place of her own to call home.

CHAPTER 32

It wasn't until after nine that night that Lisa walked in the door after finishing work. In her hand, she carried a bouquet of flowers. It was the best she could get from the grocery store nearby that was still open. "Mom? Hi! So…. I bought a house!"

Maria turned in her chair and looked at her daughter in shock. "What?.... How?... Oh Lisa, really?"

Lisa came over and put down the flowers before hugging her Mom. "It's the deal of a century Mom! I was the first person to see it and they accepted my offer!" She handed her mom the flowers, "These are for you, to celebrate the next step in our lives!"

"Oh Lisa, I'm so happy for you—and for me! This is so exciting! Tell me all about it!"

Lisa grabbed a frozen dinner and put it in the microwave while she described the house to her mom. When her meal was hot, she brought it to the chair in the living room and ate while she continued to talk. "It's going to be a ton of work, but once it's done I think we'll both be really happy, and I can easily cover the mortgage payment and then some with renting it out."

"I can't wait to see it! When did you say you get the keys?"

"The real estate agent said in a couple of days. I'm trying to figure out how long until we can move in. Probably another month or two. I have no idea how to go about getting people to work on it."

"Why don't you ask Manuel and Betsy? They sure know a lot of people. Maybe they know some contractors or something."

"That's a great idea! Oh, look, it's too late to call them tonight. I'll call them during my lunch break tomorrow. Can you even believe it? Today we were having lunch together, and by the end of the day, I bought a house! Crazy!"

They both were too excited to sleep, so Lisa got out a pen and paper and started writing down the things she thought needed doing to the house. Her mom was a good sounding board. She mostly listened, but when she did offer a suggestion, it immediately made sense to Lisa.

Lisa's 'to do' list ended up being pretty long, but if she could get her mom's room repainted and new floors put in, and her bathroom altered to be accessible, then they could move in and do the rest of the work over time. She didn't want to be paying rent and a mortgage for any longer than necessary. As soon as she had the keys to the house and had a house inspection to make sure everything was safe she'd give one month's notice at the apartment. That deadline would force her to move fast.

When she stopped for lunch the next day Lisa pulled out her phone and saw she had missed a call from Frank. She normally kept her phone on at work so her mom could get ahold of her if she needed, but in her excitement over the house she forgot to turn the ringer on in the morning. Her heart dropped as she forced herself to dial in to the voicemail. Maybe the house deal had really been too good to be true.

But happily, the voicemail confirmed that the deal was done and the house was hers. He would bring her the keys as soon as the bank finished processing the sale, probably in two days.

She called him back to say a quick thank you before calling Manuel.

He was thrilled with her news, and promised to come over with Betsy as soon as Lisa got the keys. As Maria predicted, he knew lots of people that could help Lisa get the house ready to live in. Lisa also sent texts to Janet, Amy, and Carrie to let them know her good news, and then she quickly ate her lunch so she could get back to work. She had a brand new reason to work hard—so she could put her next paycheck towards fixing up her very own house!

A few short days later Frank dropped off the keys and stayed for a cup of tea and a visit. He was so easy to talk to, and had lots of great ideas for Lisa's new house. And he noticed Maria's new hairstyle and complimented her on it. Joking that he wished he was ten years younger, Lisa burst out laughing when she saw her mom blush.

Frank also offered to ask around at the office for any recommendations for contractors. He didn't know anyone personally, but said he'd look into it further if Manuel didn't have people. When he got up to leave he promised to keep in touch. Lisa liked having him around and didn't want to lose contact. She was learning that it didn't matter how old or young someone was, if you felt a connection with them it was worth staying in contact. The friendships she enjoyed with Janet, Manuel, and Betsy were a testament to that!

March 17th dawned cold and rainy but Lisa didn't care. As soon as she was done work she'd come home and pick up her mom and take her to their new home! She barely even registered that it was her birthday, except when her mom reminded her before she left for work. Getting her own house was the best birthday gift she could imagine.

By four in the afternoon, Lisa was cleaning up her desk and walking out the door. She couldn't wait any longer! Her mom was waiting when she came home, and together they walked under an umbrella to the car.

When they arrived at the house, Lisa had to admit it looked worse than the first time she had been there! That front yard needed some help right away. Looking around at her future neighbors, it was obvious her house was the ugliest on the street. Everybody else had tidy yards and lovely landscaping.

Escaping the weather outside, she proudly showed her mom their new house. Maria even made it upstairs to look at the rooms, but Lisa said she'd wait to show her the basement until they could get it cleaned up. There was a folding table and some lawn chairs in the garage, and Lisa brought these into the dining room so they could sit and talk about the house. She brought a binder along, with lots of paper and tabs to help her keep track of everything going on with the house.

They sat for the next hour and thought out a general plan of attack, only stopping for Lisa to order pizza delivery for supper. Both agreed that tackling the front yard was a priority. Workers would need to get in with tools and supplies, and some of the shrubs would have to be removed to leave space along the front walkway. Plus, cleaning up the front and getting the garbage hauled away would probably make the neighbors feel a lot better about them!

Lisa had planned to take the solo bedroom and rent out the ones with access to bathrooms, but Maria disagreed. She felt Lisa deserved to take the master bedroom and set up her own special space there. It was the first time she really pushed Lisa for something, and she was relentless. "You gave up so many things to save for this house, you need to have the very best room! And after all those years of sharing a bathroom with roommates, and now sharing a bathroom with me it's time for you to have your own bathroom, Lisa."

"But how can I rent out that last bedroom then? Nobody will want a room where they don't have access to a bathroom! If I take that room I can share the downstairs bathroom with you. I'm not asking you to share with other people you don't even know!"

"Then put another bathroom in that room! You must have the master bedroom Lisa, you just have to!"

"Wait, Mom…that's a great idea! That room's probably big enough! And then I can charge more for it because it has a private bathroom. It's perfect!"

"And then you'll take the master bedroom?"

Lisa laughed, "I've never seen you so determined to get your own way. I like this new pushy side to you! OK, I'll take the master! Oh my goodness Mom! It will be so nice living here!"

The doorbell rang, and Lisa got up to answer it. Pizza wasn't much of a fancy dinner, but it was their first in their new home. They had just finished eating when the doorbell rang again. Manuel and Betsy were there with a beautiful potted orchid and a box with a bakery logo on it. Lisa felt like she would burst with pride as she showed them in. After a quick tour they joined Maria in the dining room and brought out cupcakes. "Your mom asked us to bring a little something over to celebrate your birthday! We are so happy for both of you!"

As they enjoyed the cupcakes, Manuel scrolled through his phone and gave Lisa names and numbers of people who could help.

He suggested Lisa hire a friend of his to come and remove some of the shrubs and tidy up the front yard so she could get a dumpster dropped off in the driveway. Then on Saturday he would come with his boys and help her clear out the garage and the front porch. Having everything clean and tidy would set a good tone for the rest of the contractors coming in.

Lisa started making calls, and lined up a few people to come in on Sunday and give her quotes for different things that needed doing. With Maria's help, she would try to manage the project herself instead of hiring someone else to do it. If things got out of hand she could bring in someone, but she wanted to control it all herself. Manuel cautioned her that she would need to spend a lot of time on site in order to make sure things ran smoothly, and Lisa agreed she'd have to keep a close eye on things.

By the time they got back to the apartment later that night, they were happy and exhausted. Maria went to bed, and Lisa made a cup of coffee and started on her freelance work. She needed to put in as much time as possible tonight and tomorrow night so she could be at the house for Saturday and Sunday. And she'd still need to work both nights on the weekend after spending the daytime at the new house. It was almost like old times when she worked two full time jobs while going to school! Only now she had what she had been working so hard for back then — her own house.

CHAPTER 33

The next day Lisa booked Manuel's friend to come and clean up the front yard. He charged $300 for the day, but promised to haul everything away so they'd have room for the dumpster coming first thing Saturday morning. Lisa met him at the house Friday after work to check things over and pay him.

The transformation was good and bad. It was wonderful to actually see the front yard and have easy access to the front door and the garage. But it also exposed the tired-looking house. At best it needed a fresh coat of paint, and at worst the siding would need to be re-done.

If this is what she could see with her own unexperienced eyes, Lisa dreaded what the home inspector would turn up next week. Oh well, she was committed now! She turned to thank the man and collect a receipt. She was planning on making money from this house, and wanted to keep close track of all the money she put into it so she could keep her taxes as low as possible.

Just as Manuel's friend was leaving, she stopped and asked if he could take a look at the back yard and quote her on tidying it up as well. She knew it would be a long time before they got to work on it, but thought perhaps some thinning out would make it easier to at least keep the lawn mown.

They went to the back yard together, and he stopped and gave a low whistle. "It's like nobody's been back here for years! You know, it's just not safe to have all this overgrowth here, especially with two ladies living alone. Anyone could sneak up to the windows without being seen!"

Well that was a new thing to worry about! "How much to just get it cleaned up?"

"$400 ma'am. I'd need to bring some help, and everything needs to be hauled to the front yard to be taken away. I'll clean up the sides of the house too."

Lisa stood and looked at the yard, and then at the painted-out basement windows that were nearly hidden by tall grass. She wanted to do it herself, but it would take her weeks, and tools she didn't own and didn't know how to use. "How soon can you come back and get it cleaned up?"

He smiled, "I'd come back tomorrow if I could have Manuel's boys to help me..."

She shook her head, "No way! They're mine tomorrow!"

"It would have to be next Saturday then. Just promise me you won't book them! They're the hardest workers I know. I tried to hire a guy a few weeks ago because it's only me, but he was so lazy it took me longer to get the job done because I was always telling him to get back to work!"

Lisa could relate to his experience. Since her promotion she had already gone through three employees that slowed the whole department down just by being there. "Could you do it for $350 next Saturday?"

He agreed, and she followed him back up through the narrow opening along the stairs on the outside of the house. It would be good to have it all cleaned up and have proper access to the whole house. Realizing it would be better for the house inspector to wait to come until after the yard was more accessible, she called and postponed his visit until the following Sunday. Then she went back to the apartment to eat a quick sandwich while she tackled her freelance work.

Maria was enjoying watching a home improvement show, and Lisa had to force herself to focus on her work instead of the TV. Normally she found it easy to pay attention to numbers over TV, but she found herself drawn into the big reno happening on TV. Tomorrow her own big reno would start!

By early afternoon on Saturday Lisa felt like she was making progress thanks to the hard work of Manuel and his boys. The garage was empty—pretty much everything just went straight into the dumpster. She was glad she had kept an old pair of jeans and a worn-out t-shirt to wear for dirty jobs, since she was filthy.

The front porch was now clear of junk and furniture and the whole yard looked much better. Lisa kept four large ceramic pots from the porch that turned out to be a very nice cream color after they were washed.

The broken garage door wasn't broken at all, only stuck because a stack of garbage had fallen on it. Once they cleared it out of the way the garage opened and closed with ease and Lisa sighed with relief that one problem was solved.

Since it took so much less time than they thought to clean out the garage and front porch, they hauled out the washer and dryer, and some garbage and broken furniture that was left in the house.

When Lisa finally stepped outside to get some fresh air, a neighbor stopped and walked up the now-cleared path.

He introduced himself as Brian, and said he lived next door with his wife Heather and their three teenagers. They were very happy to hear that Lisa had bought the house and was already fixing it up. He assured her it was a nice neighborhood and they'd all keep an eye on things for her. She hoped that meant they were friendly and not nosy. These were the people she planned on being neighbors with for a long time!

At dinnertime, Lisa insisted on everyone stopping work. Manuel and his boys had been going almost nonstop since they arrived that morning and they had more than earned the $150 she had offered for their help. Besides, she needed to get home and have a shower and do her freelance work. Tomorrow was her day to meet contractors and get the ball rolling on making the house livable, and before she even showed up she needed to go over her finances so she knew what she could afford.

When she got home her mom had prepared grilled cheese sandwiches and soup for supper. Lisa never asked for help with cooking because she found cutting anything terribly painful. Often when Lisa was late her mom would just grab a piece of bread or some crackers to eat. It was nice that she had worked through the pain to have supper for Lisa though, so she quickly showered before eating.

They agreed that Maria would join Lisa tomorrow to talk to the contractors. Lisa wanted to make sure whoever they hired could work with the two women, and would be people her mom felt comfortable with. The first appointment wasn't until eleven, so there was time for Maria to get up and ready without rushing.

Lisa found a whole new set of muscles when she woke up the next morning. This manual labor thing was brutal! It hadn't been that long ago that she stopped her janitor job, but it seemed like her body had gone soft in the meantime! She took a hot shower before making coffee, and it helped a little bit. Taking a minute to wake her mom up and get her to take her pain pills, Lisa then turned to her own finances.

Her savings account had dropped down to $26,250 after paying 25% down on the house, plus fees. It was a lot of money, but she wondered if it was enough to do the whole house. Paying to have the yard cleaned up, and for Manuel and the boys' help had already come out of her checking account, but the dumpster would cost $500 when it was hauled away. And her first mortgage payment would come out in less than a month.

By her calculations she could cover all her monthly expenses with her salary and her freelance work, even with the mortgage, house taxes, and higher utilities. What she needed was to get rooms rented out as soon as possible, so she could use that income to keep on fixing up the house. And her first mortgage payment would come out in less than a month.

She gave one month notice for the apartment so they'd be moving in here whether the house was ready or not!

Lisa and Maria were back at their new house the next morning. Maria suggested Lisa focus on getting as much of the dirty work out of the way first, so she wasn't always having to clean up. They both knew that house renovations got messy from the TV shows they watched. Lisa wrote 'take out old flooring' at the top of her list.

Fortunately, the existing upstairs bathroom just needed fresh paint and flooring. All the fixtures were in good condition, and Lisa wasn't about to rip out a bathroom just to update it. As far as Maria's bathroom, the accessibility expert would come today and let them know if they needed to make any changes to the main floor bathroom.

When the painter came to quote on painting the house, he also recommendedAt the end of the day, the ladies had a plan for their new home. Knowing that everyone they talked to had been personally recommended by Manuel helped a lot, and they quickly agreed on which people they felt would be the right ones to help them transform the h

an organization that gave troubled teens a chance to work and gain skills. He thought they could remove all the flooring from the house.

Lisa was surprised someone answered the phone when she called the number the painter had given her. First thing tomorrow morning a worker and three teens would be there to get started. Once the flooring was removed the painter would be back to start painting. Lisa and Maria needed to make some pretty quick color choices! They would also need to choose flooring as soon as possible.

Once the flooring was removed the painter would be back to start painting. Lisa and Maria needed to make some pretty quick color choices! They would also need to choose flooring as soon as possible.

According to the accessibility expert, Maria's bathroom needed some major work. The tub needed to be removed and a special shower unit put in. It would cost more to have it done through the accessibility store, but Maria wanted to use them. She insisted on paying for all the changes to the house related to accessibility. Although Lisa didn't want her mom to drain her finances, she thought handling it with her own resources would give her confidence.

It was a two week wait for the shower unit to be delivered and then a few days to install it and the grab bars around the shower and toilet.

They would also retrofit the current vanity so that Maria could pull her wheelchair right up to it, and the bathroom door needed to be widened to fit a wheelchair. Fortunately the front door and bedroom door were both wide enough for a wheelchair, and the company would install a neat little ramp that would make it easier to cross the threshold at the front door.

The plumber was the only one to give Lisa news she didn't want to hear. He strongly recommended Lisa *not* add in another bathroom upstairs. It was huge job, and would require a lot of extra demolition to access the pipes which were at the other end of the house. Lisa really didn't want to let go of the idea of having another bathroom so she could rent out that room, but when she stopped to think about it, she decided to take his advice and focus on the basement development instead. He was happy to come back and put in the plumbing for a kitchen sink after she got a permit for the basement development.

At the end of the day, they felt like they had a good plan for getting their new home fixed up. Knowing that everyone they talked to was personally recommended by Manuel helped a lot.

After all the tradespeople had been and gone, Lisa and Maria went to the home improvement store to pick out paint colors. For the main areas in the house, Lisa went with an easy soft white. In her bedroom she chose a taupe, even though her mom tried to get her to choose something more colorful.

Maria wasn't afraid of color! She chose a deep orange color for her bathroom and one wall in her bedroom, and a cream color for the rest of the walls. They decided they would invite Carrie over after the painting was done to see if she could do some bright wall hangings that would suit her mom's vibrant style.

They also chose tile for the entryway, kitchen, and bathrooms, and a durable laminate flooring for the rest of the house. Lisa couldn't wait for everything to be done so they could move in. After a quick bite to eat at the apartment she got to work on her freelancing and then went to bed early.

The next few weeks would be crazy. Maria wanted to be at the house as often as possible to keep an eye on things—it was something Manuel had stressed to them when they asked for advice. Lisa would start work at seven, leave at eleven to pick up Maria and take her to the house, and then Maria would supervise the workers until Lisa finished work and came back to pick her up. If there was a day when Maria wasn't up to being there, they'd have to figure something else out.

From the first day of work on the house Lisa was proud of the way her mom got involved with everything that was happening. She had always thought of her mom as shy and mousey, but that was only around her dad. Once Maria was out of that situation she was quite outgoing! For Lisa—who was happy to be in the background—it was a huge help. She was pretty sure nobody would get away with anything on her mom's watch!

CHAPTER 34

By the end of her first week as a homeowner, Lisa was incredibly grateful she was a bookkeeper and not a painter or a plumber, or any of the other tradespeople that had been coming in and out of the house. They all worked so hard!

The stained, old flooring had all been removed and the dumpster was so full Lisa paid for it to be emptied and then returned again. Maria loved having the teens there who were working under the supervision of a youth worker. They all started calling her "Mrs. M" and she knew them all by name.

Lisa had gotten her mom a cell phone shortly after they moved to the city, and now Maria was telling them all to keep in touch with her. One of them offered to come back and scrape all the spray paint off the windows in the basement. It would be a long and tedious job, but he insisted he had 'lots of experience' with spray paint. The worker left the final decision up to Lisa, and with her mom's encouragement, she agreed. He would come on Saturday and stay until the job was done.

Once the floors were out the painter came in. Already Maria's room was looking bright and cheerful! The demo was done in her bathroom and ready for the new shower unit, and the walls were all repainted. It took the very persistent painter three coats to cover the old paint, and he put in some long hours to get the job done on schedule.

As soon as the painter was done the floors were laid and fresh white trim installed. Room by room the house took shape. Lisa and Maria were both exhausted at the end of each day, but also happier than they had ever been before. For Lisa, she was seeing her dream take shape right in front of her eyes, and every day when she went in the house there was one more thing that was done and looking fantastic. Her biggest problem was not having time to keep up with the purchases and decisions she needed to make. Already she had a long list of stores to visit and decisions to make on Saturday when she could do some shopping.

Maria was practically glowing with this new opportunity to help her daughter out, and create a beautiful home for them both to enjoy. While in her supervisory role when Lisa was at work, she refused to back away from anyone when she saw something that needed to be done, or something that needed to be corrected. For so many years she had let Robert hurt her only child with his words, but now there was no way she would let anyone do any harm to Lisa, even if it was just splashing paint on a window and not cleaning it up!

The tradespeople all loved Maria, even when she followed behind them to make sure they were doing a good job. She knew them all by name, knew how they liked their tea or coffee (which she made for everyone every day), and always complimented them when they did a good job. She became the 'site mom'—a title she cherished. Betsy stopped by for a visit during the week and was impressed with how fast everything was coming together.

The week ended on a good note when the home inspector confirmed that there were no major problems with the house, aside from the exterior siding. Lisa was hoping to get it repainted just to make it look nice, but she learned that it needed to be repaired and painted as soon as possible because it helped to protect the house from the weather. Her painter didn't do exteriors, but he recommended someone who could. Lisa was basing every decision she made on recommendations from others. So far it was working out better than she could expect.

Her bookkeeping skills came in handy as she kept track of all the work and payments. From her own job she knew that it was important to reimburse others quickly for their expenses, and never to pay in full for a job until it was done right. Fortunately, the people working for her were all doing a great job. (She didn't find out until much later how much of a part her mom played in making sure everything was done right the first time!)

In the end, the biggest delay was Maria's bathroom because the shower surround needed to be ordered and shipped in. Everything else was completely finished—the bedrooms were all freshly painted with laminate floors, the bathrooms were painted and the tile was finished, and the rest of the house was also painted. Lisa loved walking into her new house and feeling a sense of brightness and optimism. She found herself walking around the house touching things like the new trim around the windows, or the beautiful stainless steel appliances she chose, or even just standing and looking at the bright orange accent wall in her mom's bedroom.

The floor installer asked if Lisa was interested in hiring his wife to come and clean the whole house when the construction was done. Lisa was dreading that job because she just didn't have any extra time or energy, and she quickly agreed. It took two days for her to clean everything, but the finished result was well worth it. She suspected the young couple was having a hard time financially, and hoped the $200 for the housecleaning helped them out. Every surface sparkled and Lisa was pretty sure there wasn't a speck of dust in the whole house! Even the basement windows were washed inside and out, and they could finally go down there and appreciate all the natural light that flooded the basement in the mornings. It would be a really nice place for someone once it was finished.

It wasn't until everything in the main areas of the house was done that Lisa felt ready to tackle the basement development. She needed to draw up a plan and get a development permit from city hall, and it felt too overwhelming to do when everything else was going on. It took some time, but she found good resources online that helped her prepare the right information for the application.

The second Friday in April, Lisa took her drawings to city hall during her lunch break to get a building permit. After almost an hour waiting she had her appointment, and within minutes she was back out, with a promise that she'd receive approval in about two weeks. It was a relief to know she had time to pack and move her and her mom before taking on the next challenge.

Saturday morning Lisa was up early working on her freelance jobs. She was just barely keeping up, and was looking forward to being settled in the new place so she could start working ahead of deadlines instead of right to them!

Once her mom was up and moving, they ate breakfast and then started packing up. Manuel and his boys were coming with a rental truck after lunch, and with a bit of luck they'd spend tonight in their new home! Lisa was so pleased with the cleaner that the same lady would be coming to the apartment tomorrow to clean it before they gave back the keys. It was another job Lisa was happy to pass on.

Lisa and Maria laughed at how many more clothes they had than when they first moved into the apartment. Somehow they continued to find some time to shop in between everything else that was going on! When Manuel and the boys arrived, everything that could be bagged or boxed was ready to go, and it was just a matter of loading things up and going to the new house.

That night Lisa lay in her single bed feeling a bit like a tiny island in the big master bedroom. Her thoughts were all over the place; thinking about getting renters as soon as possible, making lists of all the things to do in the basement, wondering how to make such a big house feel cozier, and still trying to come to grips with the fact that *she* owned *this* house. It was a lot to take in.

She woke up with sunlight streaming in the windows. One of the things she had completely forgotten about was window coverings, so last night she had quickly tacked up a sheet over her window and her mom's window to give them some privacy. It would have been nice to spend the whole day in the house, but there was still shopping to do.

After a quick shower in her beautiful bathroom (and a little thought of thanks that her mom had insisted she take this space for her own), she dried her hair and pulled on a pair of blue jeans and a yellow t-shirt with a white band around the neck and arms. She went downstairs to start her freelancing while the coffee brewed. But instead she stood at the sliding doors in the dining room looking out over the view. The morning sun was almost too bright but Lisa didn't mind, and it highlighted a decent sized back yard.

Even from upstairs she could see the lilac bush blooming in the back corner. It needed trimming, but it was nice there was some color in the yard already. She didn't recognize the single tree that was there, but it had a nice shape to it. Just beside the lilac was a cheap metal shed she hadn't been able to open yet.

After the yard was cleared, Lisa took a quick wander to see what was there. The fence around the yard looked battered and was missing a few boards here and there. She could see that the neighbor on the right had their own fence beside hers, but on the left they were stuck sharing a fence. Added onto her mental list was to talk to the neighbors—she was sure they'd like to have less of an eyesore—and to buy a lawnmower and trimmer soon. It was important that she keep the yard at least looking tidy until she had time and money to spruce it up.

Money was another 'to do' on her list, and an important one. She kept a running total of all the expenses, and after paying Manuel and the boys yesterday for their help moving, she had just over $11,000 left in her savings. When the exterior painting was done later that week, she'd have to pay out another $1,800. The funds had gone out pretty fast in the past few weeks, but she kept reminding herself that her account would recover when she had rooms rented out.

With her coffee and her laptop set up at the table she pushed all other thoughts to the side and got to work on her freelancing. At nine she took a quick break to make sure her mom was awake and had taken her morning pills, and then grabbed another cup of coffee and kept working. An hour later, Maria surprised Lisa by joining her.

She said a cheery good morning before turning the kettle on for a cup of tea. "How did you sleep in your big bedroom?"

"I actually felt a little weird at first. My bed felt so small! But it was good, really good. How about you?"

"Oh Lisa, I had such a good sleep! And it was so nice to use the bathroom without help in the morning. They did a good job of my bathroom, didn't they?"

Lisa had to admit, having the right supports in the bathroom sure made a difference. And she was relieved that her mom could do more on her own now. That would be good for both of them.

Once Maria had her cup of tea, Lisa put away her work and got out her phone to make a list for their day. She needed to get measurements for the windows so they could get blinds and maybe buy a lawnmower and trimmer. It would be nice if she could find something used. She had a feeling that all the extras they needed for the house could swallow up the rest of her cash if she wasn't careful.

Later that afternoon they were back at home, and Lisa was bracing herself to use a drill for the first time. The man who served them at the home improvement store assured Lisa the blinds they chose were easy to install and she could do it herself, even if it was her first time. She read the instructions three times before carefully starting. Three hours later she had installed blinds in the upstairs bedrooms and her mom's bedroom. They both agreed that they had made an excellent choice, and Lisa was quite proud to have her first DIY under her belt.

That night she was up late finishing her freelancing. She was looking forward to getting back to her usual schedule so she wouldn't have to pull such long hours in the evenings. But at least she had kept her clients happy!

CHAPTER 35

At work the next day, Lisa saw a hand-written note on the employee bulletin board from someone selling some furniture. It took her to the planning department where she found the lady who posted the notice. June's daughter was moving out of the country and needed to sell almost all her furniture immediately.

"Here, I've got pictures of almost everything on my phone. She's got this big job in the middle east. I wish she wasn't going so far away!"

Lisa looked through the pictures—it looked like she could use almost everything there, and June said her husband could deliver everything for an extra fee.

The next day Lisa rode with June to her daughter's house. It really felt like she had hit the jackpot! There was everything for two complete bedrooms, plus a three-seater cream colored sofa with green accent pillows, an area rug, and a table and chairs to seat six.

Lisa thought the value of everything was probably well over $2,000 even though it was used. It all looked high quality, and nearly new. But before she could make an offer, the daughter suggested $1,000 for everything including delivery if Lisa would take it right away.

She quickly agreed, and arranged a time the next evening to have everything brought to the house.

As she rode the bus home from June's daughter's house, Lisa tried to put her decreasing savings account out of her mind. She knew she should be glad that she could do so much right away, Traffic ended up bringing the bus to a halt, and Lisa could see some sort of minor accident ahead that was blocking the road. She sent her mom a quick text to say she was stuck in traffic, and then sat back and closed her eyes. It was nice to have a few minutes to breathe... Seconds later her eyes popped open again.

Airbnb! She was going to look into renting out one room with Airbnb and had totally forgotten. A lady that worked a few desks down from her started doing it about a month ago, and said it brought in more money than a regular tenant would, and she never worried about being stuck living with someone she didn't care for, since most of the guests only stayed for a night or two. Lisa decided to look into it that night after she finished her freelance work.

The next night Lisa helped June's husband and daughter bring in all the furniture she had bought. She had already moved her single bed into one of the other bedrooms and was taking the 'new' queen sized bed as her own. They moved the furniture into the house and surprised Lisa with some nice framed IKEA prints that would look great in the extra bedrooms.

When they left Lisa realized she didn't have bedding for a queen bed! She borrowed an extra set of sheets from her mom, and put her old blankets back on her new bed. She'd have to buy more bedding right away, but then she'd have enough for one of the rooms so she could set it up with Airbnb.

During her lunch break Lisa went out and quickly bought a bedding set for her bed, and some extra pillows and towels for the other rooms. It would be awkward bringing it all home on the bus, but she didn't want to have to make another shopping trip over the weekend if she could help it.

Saturday morning she set up the one bedroom and took pictures so she could put her first listing on Airbnb. The finished room looked really nice, and she added in some pictures of the kitchen and a close up of the kettle and coffee maker. When she looked at other rooms on Airbnb in her area she was surprised to see them priced anywhere from $75 to $109 per night for a single bedroom. That seemed high, so she settled on $65 per night. She could always change the price later.

Knowing what she had been looking for when she rented a room, she listed things like distance to the nearest bus stop, free Wi-Fi, semi-private bathroom, and her favorite city parks and restaurants. Maria joined her just as she was about to submit her listing, and Lisa walked her through the process.

"Lisa, I was thinking that I'd like to learn to use a computer. Maybe if I do that I'll find some sort of job I can do. Now that the house is set up I want to keep busy."

Lisa thought it was a great idea, and looked up classes in the area. They were surprised to see there was one at a library branch nearby that started today. With all the busyness of getting the house fixed up, they hadn't even explored their neighborhood. It looked to be a five minute walk away, and Maria wanted to give it a try. Lisa reluctantly agreed, with the promise that Maria would text if she had trouble or needed a ride. As she walked out the door an hour later Lisa felt a bit like a parent saying goodbye to their child on the first day of school. She was even tempted to follow her, just to make sure she was OK!

Instead she got her work out and tried to focus. She wanted to have tomorrow completely free to do things in the yard instead of having to get more work done first. When Maria walked in the door two hours later Lisa was shocked that so much time had passed! She offered to make her a cup of tea while she settled into her special chair.

"Whew! That's more walking than I've done in a long time! My whole body hurts!"

"Do you think you did too much Mom?"

"I think I won't know until I try to get up... The class was lovely though. I was the youngest one there which was a nice change. I think I'd like to get my own computer—one like yours, maybe. How much did yours cost?"

"I bought mine on sale for $800, but I think you could get something cheaper..."

The kettle whistled and Lisa poured hot water into her mom's favorite floral mug. She waited a minute before taking out the tea bag and adding milk and sugar. Then she grabbed a packet of cookies from the cupboard and brought everything over to the TV tray that sat beside her mom's chair in the living room. They planned on getting more furniture at some point, but things worked for now. Having the couch certainly made the room feel more comfortable, especially with the area rug with its soft swirls of color.

Lisa went back to get her laptop from the table and then sat on the couch with her legs tucked up. "You know, we should try to do more stuff online. I'm getting really tired of going into stores every weekend."

"Well, maybe after I've learned a bit more and gotten my own computer I can help with that!"

They looked at some different options, and Maria chose a laptop with good reviews. She only had a small secured credit card similar to what Lisa had gotten years ago, so Lisa put the laptop on her credit card and her mom wrote her a check to pay her back.

Maria looked up from her checkbook, "Oh, I called Carrie yesterday, remember that lady we met at the play place? I left a message asking if she could do some framed pictures for my bedroom. She texted back that she was just in the middle of final exams and would pop over to see what I wanted when she was done. Probably the beginning of May. That must be quite the challenge, taking exams while raising two kids. I hope she does well."

"They seemed like such nice kids." Maria reached over and picked up the TV remote. They were both hooked on watching home improvement shows and it was a nice way to unwind at the end of the day. But Lisa wanted to get a few more things done before relaxing.

"I think now that the painter's moved to the back of the house it's time to get some flowers in front. Remember what a difference it made when Kathleen brought her pots of flowers over when we sold your house? I'll use the pots that were on the front porch when we got here first, and hopefully there's some more things in that shed that we can use for the deck. You're welcome to come with me to buy plants."

"Nope, I think I'm good and truly stuck here for a while. In fact, can you bring me a pill?"

Lisa brought her mom a pain pill and a glass of water. She hoped the trip to the library hadn't been too much, but there seemed to be no way to tell in advance what was, or wasn't too much with RA. And sometimes what was fine one day wasn't fine the next. It was an exercise in always trying to be flexible, in case they had to change their plans.

She checked on the painter before leaving to buy soil and plants. He figured he still had another hour and a half to go before he was done, and Lisa promised to be back by then to pay him. The whole house was looking miles better. He had scraped any old or chipped paint first, and then painted the house a cream color, with dark green trim and it looked really sharp. The final touch was a dark red paint for the front door which Lisa loved.

It was dusk when she finished with the pots. They all had pretty little trailing white flowers around the edges, with deep purple and bright yellow flowers in the center. Another neighbor walked by and stopped to visit. He told Lisa that they were delighted with every-thing she had done already to the place, and everyone was looking forward to meeting them at the annual neighborhood BBQ they had the first Saturday in July. It was the first Lisa had heard of it but she promised she and her mom would join them. That would be the perfect way to meet everyone around them and make more friends. Lisa was still surprised at how friendly and outgoing her mom was now. Just went to show how who you lived with could change everything about how you acted.

CHAPTER 36

Sunday morning Lisa was surprised to sleep in. Normally she was awake early on the weekends to get stuff done, but things had caught up with her body. Well, that, plus her new queen sized bed was really comfortable, and her new blinds kept the morning light out until she was ready to let it in.

She peeked in to say good morning to her mom who was sitting in bed reading a book she had gotten from the library, and then sat with a coffee to check her email. She was shocked to see there was already an inquiry from Airbnb! A lady coming to the city for a work contract wanted to book the room for four nights, beginning tonight! Quickly Lisa approved the booking and then went to tell Maria the good news.

It felt like she should be running around doing something to get ready, but there wasn't really anything to do. The bathroom and bedroom were all set up, she had extra tea and coffee and some things for breakfast if the guest wanted. Lisa clipped a few little branches of lilacs to put in a vase in the bathroom, and then put chocolates and a bottle of water on the night table and she was ready.

An email popped up with a short message that Leanne would be arriving between seven and eight that evening.

With the rest of the day ahead of her, Lisa and Maria enjoyed a leisurely late breakfast, and then Lisa went out to the shed in the back yard. She was determined to get it opened today and cleaned out so she could store her new electric lawnmower in there instead of the garage. Then she would spend the rest of the day working on the yard.

Armed with a small crowbar, a hammer, and some pliers, Lisa tackled the shed. It was metal, about six feet long and three feet wide with two sliding doors that joined at the center. There wasn't a lock or anything keeping the doors closed, so she figured they were either jammed by something that had fallen against them inside the shed, or stuck from years of not being used. Since the shed wasn't even visible the first time they came, she didn't think it had been used for quite a long time.

The left side seemed to give a bit when she wiggled it, and it squealed in protest as she slowly opened it one inch at a time. When the opening was big enough to get her arm through, she turned on her phone's flashlight and took a look around. It was full of junk, and some boards had fallen against the right door. Squeezing as much of herself into the opening as possible, she managed to move the boards away. Then using her body and both hands she wiggled the left door up and down until it was almost completely open.

Once the sun could shine into the shed, it didn't look too bad. There were some long cobwebs hanging down, but it looked like everything was actually fairly well organized. She took the boards out and leaned them up against the fence. On one side was an old canvas tarp which she slowly pulled off, trying not to shake dust everywhere. Underneath were stacks of picture frames, some with paintings in them, and some empty. Right away she thought of Carrie—she could probably use them.

Lisa decided the frames needed to go into the house so she went inside and down to the basement and opened the sliding doors.

Many of the frames were at least two feet long, and felt solid. The few paintings were beautiful landscapes with soft colors. She immediately decided to clean them up and hang them inside. The house needed some decoration and the price sure was right!

After all the frames were inside she went back and cleaned out the rest of the shed. There were some good quality gardening tools, and three rectangular planters that would be perfect for the deck, just as she hoped. There was also the required cookie tin full of nails (did every shed have one of these?), and another square tin that was stuffed with old pictures and letters. Lisa put that aside to bring upstairs and look at later.

She gave the entire shed a good sweeping and was pleased to see she could easily fit the lawnmower and trimmer, freeing up space in the garage. After all the other tools were put back she went and got the lawnmower out and mowed the lawn. Even though it was a job she had hated as a child, doing it in her own yard was completely different. It made the yard instantly look better, especially once she edged everything.

Trimming the shrubs wouldn't be quite so easy. The guy who came when she first bought the house had done a great job of taking care of the overgrowth, but there was still a ways to go to get the neat and tidy look Lisa was imagining.

She started with two that were on either side of the living room window and were starting to block the sun. Lisa was ruthless, cutting them down to less than half their size. Either they'd be grateful for their new look, or they'd die and she'd pull them out. By the time she cleaned up all the trimmings and put everything away, she was starving.

Maria put a small roast and some potatoes in the oven for supper. It wasn't Amy's over-the-top roast beef dinner, but it was still delicious after a busy day. Maria was managing in her new bathroom on her own, and with Amy's encouragement they agreed to a trial without her help. While they were both thrilled with Maria's independence they missed Amy's cheerful presence. Lisa decided to give her a call after supper.

"Lisa! How did you know I needed to chat?" Amy sounded different, although Lisa couldn't quite place what was different.

"Oh, I was just thinking about you and decided to call. How are things?"

Amy sighed, "Not good. Aunt Helena stopped eating two days ago. It won't be long now."

"You mean... she's..." Lisa didn't know how to say it.

"Dying?" Amy offered. "Yeah... there's a nurse here all the time now, and family are coming in from out of town."

"So, how are you?"

"I'm just so sad! She's become my whole life in the past year, and I don't know what I'll do when she's gone. I know she's ready to go, but I'm not ready for her to go!"

"I'm so sorry Amy. Is there anything I can do? Do you need a break? You're welcome to come over here! We've got lots of room, even lots of bedrooms!"

"I might just take you up on that, thanks. For now I just need to stick around. But after... I don't want to stay here after."

Lisa promised to keep the second bedroom open for Amy, and told her to call at any time if she needed anything. She hung up feeling sad herself. Aunt Helena was so full of life the last time Lisa had seen her. Even though she was well into her 90s, it seemed strange to think of her as getting ready to die.

Her thoughts were interrupted by the doorbell. It was Leanne, her very first Airbnb guest. Lisa and Maria both met her at the door and welcomed her. After showing her to her room, Lisa left her to get settled and invited her to come down if she was interested in a cup of tea, or needed anything.

A little while later she joined them, and Lisa felt like it was almost the same as having roommates, with everyone chatting in the living room and getting to know each other. Leanne often traveled for work, and found that Airbnb's operated by women provided a safer, more comfortable stay than hotels, and were almost always less expensive. Since Lisa only had one experience traveling she hadn't thought of that, and decided to change the wording on her listing a bit to reflect this.

CHAPTER 37

On Friday Amy's Aunt Helena passed away. Amy showed up at Lisa's door with tears in her eyes, carrying a small backpack and a pillow. "I'm sorry, I should've called, but I just needed to get away from everything. Mom knows I'm here."

Lisa welcomed her with a big hug and showed her upstairs. "Here, this room isn't quite as put together as the other one, but it's yours for as long as you want it." She had just put sheets and a blanket on it the day before, and was glad it was ready for Amy. They walked downstairs together and Lisa put on the kettle. She'd have to remember to stock up on tea, as everyone who came in the door seemed to prefer it.

Amy joined Maria in the living room and Lisa brought her tea over. "Did you want to talk about it?" Maria asked.

Amy shook her head. "I just want to be here. I have to go back to the house tomorrow, that's where everyone wants to visit."

"Well I'm sure Lisa has already told you you're welcome to stay here for as long as you want. We had a lovely lady here for most of the week, Leanne. Lisa has that other room on Airbnb. It's nice having more people around!"

They had a quiet evening watching TV and having small conversations about little things. Amy commented on the landscape that Lisa had hung up already. "Can you believe that was just sitting in the shed? It a miracle it wasn't damaged by the weather or anything. There's two more, one's in my bedroom and I think I'll hang the other in the hallway after I've cleaned it."

Saturday Lisa got a request for a last-minute Airbnb booking for just the one night, but she hardly noticed the extra guest. After letting her in around nine pm, she was back out the door Sunday morning before anyone was up. Leanne had already left a nice review for the room and promised to book again if she was in the city.

The rest of the weekend passed quietly. Lisa worked, gardened, and cleaned the house—way more work in a bigger house. Maria went to her second computer class at the library (although Lisa insisted on picking her up after) and came home with a list of new friends to keep in touch with. Amy spent nights at the house and appreciated the peace and quiet when she could be there.

Now that Lisa wasn't paying rent *and* a mortgage she was seeing her savings account go up instead of down—although that would change again when she started finishing the basement. The development permit came through after just a week, but she was still waiting to hear back from the different people who would do the work.

And in the meantime, her one little room on Airbnb had done better than expected. If she could have someone there just ten days a month, it would generate the same income as having a permanent renter there. Maria was learning to use her new laptop, and offered to help Lisa out with responding to inquiries and even checking guests in if Lisa was at work.

She took the afternoon off work for Aunt Helena's funeral, and couldn't help but compare her dad's funeral—with two people—to this funeral where the church was packed with people who had loved the fiery lady. There were so many people around Amy afterwards that Lisa quietly slipped out. She'd be available for Amy later if she needed to talk. It was a good thing she hadn't put up a listing to rent out that room yet. Even though she wasn't getting the income from it, being able to provide that space for her friend was worth far more to her.

When Amy arrived back at the house that night, she just gave Maria and Lisa a quick wave and went to her room. But the next morning she was at the table when Lisa came down.

Lisa went to start the coffee and put on the kettle for Amy. "Hey, how are you doing?"

"I'm OK. Thanks. Now that the funeral's over I feel like I can breathe a little. I hate funerals."

They sat for a few minutes until the coffee was ready and Lisa brought over mugs for each of them. "You know you can stay here for as long as you like. There's no rush to make any decisions. The past year Aunt Helena was almost your whole life. I think that will take some time to deal with."

"Actually, about two weeks ago we had a long talk about my future. I think she knew it was her time or something. I still want to take nursing, so I'm going to apply to start in September."

Lisa smiled and reached over to hug her friend, "Oh Amy, that's fantastic! You'll be such a great nurse!"

"The only thing is, I'll need a place to stay. Aunt Helena's house is for sale, and she's left me enough money to pay for schooling and room and board somewhere. I don't suppose you know of anyone looking for a roommate?" She gave Lisa a mischievous smile, the first smile Lisa had seen in days.

"Are you serious? I'd love to have you here! Oh my goodness, how lucky am I? What's your budget for rent? I want to help however I can!"

"That place where we met was charging $600 per month, and your house is way nicer. How about $750?"

Lisa just about choked on her coffee, "$750? Not a chance! That's way too much. I'll do $600 and not a dollar more! Oh boy, look at the time. I've gotta go or I'll be late! Can you check on mom in a bit if she's not up? Thanks roomie!"

Lisa practically danced to the bus stop. Amy would be a perfect roommate. She already fit in like she was family, and the house wouldn't feel so big and empty with someone else living there.

On the bus, she took a call from the man who had been recommended to frame out the rooms in the basement. He could come by in the evening to give a quote, but wouldn't be able to start until the following weekend. Everyone told her how lucky she was to get the rest of the house fixed up in such a short amount of time, so she'd have to be patient with the basement work, but she really wanted to have it done and making money as soon as possible.

CHAPTER 38

The beginning of May brought flowers, guests, and workers coming in and out of the basement as it slowly took shape. The two shrubs that Lisa had nearly chopped down in the front yard were rewarding everyone with huge blue hydrangea blooms, and it inspired Lisa to continue to cut back the rest of the front yard growth. Underneath most of it she found tulips popping up through the soil and she couldn't wait to see what sorts of colors they'd be.

Downstairs, the two bedrooms were framed out, the cabinets and counter for the little kitchen were in, and the electrical and plumbing were finished. Over the next week a drywaller would come in the evenings and he hoped finish by Sunday night. Lisa waited to confirm the painter until the drywall was complete and dry but if everything worked out she'd be ready to start renting it out before June. She felt fortunate that the house was already zoned for a basement suite, and with the electrical inspection done she only had to have the inspector in one more time when everything was finished before she could legally rent it out.

Amy took a full-time job as a care aide at the care home she used to work at until she started school. Although she was often working the evening shift, on the times that she was home at dinner time the three women would stick around after eating and visit.

Amy's mom was quite involved in Amy's life when they first met as roommates. Lisa still remembered her first impression of Sandra as a powerful force tearing through the house and demanding the best for her daughter. She had paid Amy's rent for her until Amy moved in with her Aunt Helena. But after living with her aunt for a month she realized the importance of taking control of her life completely.

Since then she had made ends meet with the fee her aunt insisted on paying her, and some casual work at the care home. Now she was trying to figure out how to continue getting ahead financially while going to school full-time. Lisa's own experience was inspiring, simply because of all she had accomplished in the past five years and Amy wanted to create her own success story.

Maria did a lot more listening than talking during these conversations. She was so proud of her daughter and of Amy for taking control of their finances and their futures and she often told them so. What she didn't share with them was her own dream to finally have an income. It was nice to have this place to stay with Lisa, and to have been able to pay for the renovations to her space. But that money had come from her late husband, even if it was unintentional on his part. She wanted to earn her own money, too. There were a few people in the computer class at the library that she suspected were in a similar position.

Meanwhile, work progressed in the basement. When the painter was nearly finished, Lisa felt confident in booking the floor layer and speaking to his wife who had already done two rounds of cleaning for her. Carla was grateful for the offer to clean the basement, and could be available on short notice. Again, Lisa got the impression that she and her husband were in a tight spot and could use any help they could get.

It was a good thing that Lisa had the work in the basement and her freelance work to keep challenging her. While she still loved her job at Golden Lion International, she wasn't finding it as challenging as she used to. She was past her two year mark with the company and had the department she was responsible for operating smoothly and efficiently. But now that she had sorted out their earlier challenges, she found her days were a bit too routine.

When she was waitressing and working as a janitor most of the job was the same, but there were always surprises and challenges that came up and kept her on her toes. Now, the workdays seemed to go by slower and slower.

She tried to think positively. Her salary was excellent for a book-keeper with her experience. She had a good pension plan with employer matching. Technically she also had extended medical benefits, although she never used them. And she had two weeks of holidays that she could take if she wanted to… What she really needed was a new challenge.

Just then her mom showed her a text from Carrie, the lady who she wanted to order some wall hangings from:

> *Hi Maria! This is Carrie. Sorry to take so long to get back to you, but I'd love to visit you and Lisa, and maybe see about some wall hangings. When's a good time?*

That would be nice! Maybe Carrie could help her figure out how to keep moving forward in life. Maria replied that anytime Saturday or Sunday was fine, and to bring the kids along. They agreed on Saturday at two in the afternoon. Lisa knew her mom would be happiest about the kids coming over. She made a mental note to pick up some kid-friendly foods when she got groceries.

Just as Lisa thought, her mom was excited about having kids over. If only she had a sibling who could produce lots of grandbabies for her mom to spoil! Oh well, maybe Carrie would let them borrow her kids once in a while.

CHAPTER 39

It was late Saturday morning when Carla came to clean the basement suite. Lisa was thrilled with the way it had turned out. There was one large bedroom, one single bedroom, a good sized living/dining area that faced the backyard, and a cute little kitchenette and bathroom. She planned on listing it for $1,250 as soon as she could get blinds on the windows and take pictures.

Carla agreed with Lisa about how nice everything looked. Even though her husband had been the one to lay the new floors, he hadn't told her much about the place. Lisa mentioned that her friend and two kids were coming over and warned her that the kids might head into the backyard for a bit.

"Oh, do you like kids?" Carla asked.

"Sure I do. But it's my mom who loves them. I think she's very sad I'm not popping out babies. And there mostly seems to be teenagers in this neighborhood so she's out of luck there! Well, I'll leave you to it, but please feel free to come upstairs if you want to take a tea or coffee break or need anything."

When Carrie arrived, Lisa had fun showing her around her house.

Carrie couldn't get over how good everything looked and how quickly she had turned it around. And she was really impressed with the frames Lisa found in the shed. "I've never worked with frames this big before. They're fantastic! I can definitely do something with them and give your mom some options for her room. How much would you like for the rest of the frames?"

"Well, since you're doing me a favor by taking them off my hands, I don't think you should pay me for them!"

"Alright, I'll take the frames and bring you back a finished picture for your mom's room and we'll call it even." They agreed, and went back downstairs where Maria was sitting at the kitchen table giggling with Matthew and Katie, Carrie's kids. Matthew had his short brown hair combed neatly to the side, and was wearing a button up shirt—on a Saturday! Katie was wearing colorful hair clips that held her curly brown hair off her face, a long sleeved pink t-shirt with a short sleeved green t-shirt overtop, and a rainbow colored tutu over jeans. They couldn't be more opposite, except for their round faces and their soft brown eyes that were exactly like their mom's.

Already the kids were enjoying juice and cookies, and Lisa offered Carrie tea or coffee. "Coffee please."

"Finally! Another coffee lover! Carrie, you would not believe how many people prefer tea to coffee. It's crazy!"

Carrie agreed. She sat at the table and looked outside. "Wow, you've really done well to get this place! The views from every window are beautiful. So much green, and so much color. It's like my dream house, right here!"

"Do you have plans to move then?" Maria asked.

"Not for a while yet. I've got two years of grad school coming up, and then probably six months of working in a practicum situation before I can start generating a regular salary. Of course, doing the picture frames really helps with the finances, but I need more than that to get a mortgage."

Lisa told her about her situation, and how much a mortgage broker helped with getting her first house. Carrie added Sandra's number into her phone right away.

"You know, I'm realizing that you never can tell when the next good thing is around the corner! Last year I was—" she paused and looked at her kids, before continuing, "—let's say in a tough situation that I couldn't see an end to. And now I'm getting ready for grad school!"

Lisa agreed, "When I moved to the city I was just focused on covering my expenses every month. I didn't have any plans for a career or any sort of future. Then I met Janet and found out that I could actually get a job where I played with numbers all day! It was perfect!"

Maria interrupted, "You didn't just go from one to the other though, you've had a few transformations along the way."

"Transformations…" Carrie looked thoughtful. "I like that. Transformations. As women, we're never just one thing, are we? Or, if we are one thing for a time, it transforms into something new or extra. What about you Maria? What's your transformation?"

"Oh, I should answer this one!" Lisa laughed, "Mom has transformed from a shadow of a woman to the proverbial popular girl! She makes friends wherever she goes, and loves being surrounded by people. I never would have expected this side to her. And when we were doing the renovations to the house? She was here every day, making sure everything went smoothly. There were some teenage boys here at the beginning on some sort of parole work thing, and mom is still in contact with them, right mom?"

"Oh, just the one boy. Shawn MacPherson. He's the one who came back to scrape all the spray paint off the windows in the basement. A good kid, he's just had trouble adjusting to his mom leaving. But it sounds like he's doing alright now. He texts when he's feeling down and we talk through it."

"See what I mean? She's totally transformed!"

Carrie agreed. She liked this pair who had beaten the odds to create a good relationship, even though the past had not been good for them. She hoped she could be a part of more lives like this when she was a psychologist. Human nature was so amazing when you gave it a little chance to thrive!

The kids were starting to get fidgety, and Carrie suggested they should get going. Just as they got up, Carla came in from the basement.

"Hello!" Carrie responded, "You look so familiar!"

"Carrie, meet Carla," Lisa introduced them, "Carla's husband laid all the floors in the house, and Carla's rescued me from piles of drywall dust! Carla, this is Carrie and her kids Matthew and Katie —"

"You're Becky's mom." Matthew interrupted.

Instantly, Carla's face lit up. "Yes, that's right. How do you know Becky?"

"Becky comes to music class with us." He turned to his mom, "Becky's the one who's special needs, Mom. I told you about her. She's nice."

"Ohhh, that's where I recognize you from! Our kids go to the same school, I've seen you dropping off your daughter!"

Carla reached out to shake Carrie's hand. "Nice to meet you!" She turned to Matthew, "And thanks for knowing Becky's name. Most kids just try to ignore her."

"She's alright," Matthew responded, suddenly shy. "I try to say hi to her during class. I think she tries to say hi back."

"She probably does," Carla assured him, "She really likes being around other kids, and she's pretty good at noticing the friendly kids. If she makes eye contact with you, that's one way she says hello."

"Cool!" Matthew responded, "I'll say hi again this week then."

As Carrie and her kids got ready to head out the door, Carla held back. Once all the big frames and the kids were loaded in Carrie's Honda, they all said goodbye. Lisa thought the house immediately felt a bit empty.

"How old is your daughter?" Maria asked Carla.

"She's eleven now. But she functions at a much lower level. Probably two or three years old. It's so nice to hear another child in school knows who she is. Sometimes I worry that she's invisible to everyone."

"Does she go to school full-time then?"

"Yes, she's got an aide at school who helps out. We're still trying to figure out how best to help her, since we just moved here in September... Anyways, I wanted to ask you something." She turned to Lisa.

"Of course! What do you need?"

"Well, I was wondering... and you can say no, that's totally fine. I just... um, do you have a renter for the basement yet?"

"No, I didn't want to advertise until I could take pictures and list it properly. Why? Do you know someone who's looking for a place?"

"Yeah... well, it's us. Chris and Becky and me. I totally understand if you're not comfortable with it. And we... so, we don't have very good credit..."

There was something about Carla that seemed so sincere, and yet so insecure. Lisa wasn't quite sure how to reassure her until her mom stepped in.

"Sounds like something for a cup of tea. Lisa, could you put the kettle on? And Carla, come have a seat and tell us everything."

CHAPTER 40

Carla sat at the table and fidgeted with the worn cuff on her sleeve for a minute before talking. "We—Chris and I—had a company. A construction company. But with the economy tanking, people started taking longer and longer to pay us. It didn't seem like a big deal at first, and we didn't want to hurt people who were having such a hard time by insisting they pay us, or going to collections or anything… but then we got behind ourselves." Carla quickly wiped away the tears that were now trickling down her face. Lisa brought over the tea and sat down beside her quietly.

"We lost everything. Our business, our home, everything. Chris' parents said we could come live with them until we got back on our feet, and we didn't feel like we had a choice. But his dad can't stand Becky. He's always making comments about how stupid she is, and how we should force her to talk, and how it's my fault she is the way she is. It's not fair to Becky and I can't take it anymore.

Chris has been working wherever he can, and I have too, but our credit is so bad we can't even rent a single bedroom apartment! And we just… we have to get out soon. Becky can't tell me how she feels but I can see it in her eyes. We spend all our time there in the bedroom we share, or we just go out walking for hours. Your place downstairs, it's so beautiful. And it feels so peaceful here. I promise you, we'll never be late on the rent, and Chris can help you with anything you need around the house! But according to the bank we're 'high risk'..."

Maria's eyes were pooling with tears as she listened to Carla, but all Lisa felt was anger. How dare that man speak such horrible things to a child! And treat Carla and Chris so badly after they had been through so much!

"Are you done cleaning Carla?" Lisa asked gently.

"What? Oh, sorry, yes, just about. I just wanted to come up for a glass of water. I'm so sorry. I don't mean to unload on you. I think Matthew's little thing about knowing Becky kinda made me all mushy for a minute. If you want to check that everything's OK I'll be going..."

"No Carla, that's not what I mean. I wanted to know if it's ready for you to move in. You can come tonight if you want. You need to get Becky out of there, and we'll do whatever we can to help. My mom and I spent a lot of years with a mean man, so we know what it's like."

Carla looked from Lisa to Maria in shock, struggling to come up with something to say. "That's so nice of you. But, what would you want for rent?"

"Would you be willing to help us out upstairs with some house-cleaning every month? I'm having trouble keeping up with this big house and I could really use some help."

"Yes, of course! Anything you want!"

"Then I suggest $1,000 per month, starting in June. You can move in right away, and we'll credit all the cleaning you've done already for the rest of this month's rent."

Carla started to really cry then, and Lisa and Maria gave her a few minutes to let it all out. Then Maria spoke up, "Carla, honey, your little girl is your special treasure. It would be an honor to share the house with her and her parents. Let us help you a little bit here, and maybe you could share her with us once in a while? It would be lovely to have some little visitors!"

Carla laughed through her tears, "OK, let me call Chris."

It was emotional for everyone to hear Carla tell her husband there was a place where they were all welcome. He agreed that they could move to Lisa's as soon as Carla came back with the truck. Before she left, Lisa grabbed a bunch of flattened boxes and a tape gun that had been sitting in the garage since they had moved in. Carla smiled through her tears, and promised they would be back in a few hours.

As soon as she left, Maria was on the ball. "Quick Lisa! Let's go to that superstore and stock the kitchen. I want to have a big welcome ready for them when they get back."

Lisa ran to her room to get her purse, and together mom and daughter set out. She felt relieved, fulfilled, and that this was the *right* thing to do. Until the moment that Carla talked about her father-in-law, Lisa had felt sorry for them, but nothing else. Hearing that someone was verbally abusing another girl set off a switch inside of her. *This* was something she could do something about!

They had fun filling their cart with food, treats for Becky, a few microwave dinners, a microwave, and a little space heater, just in case it was too cold in the basement for Becky. Just when they were about finished, Maria suggested they get helium balloons and a bouquet of tulips with a vase.

Back at home Lisa took everything downstairs and organized it all in the kitchen. Now that everything was clean and the construction dust was gone, the place felt warm and cozy. It was the perfect place for the little family to recover from the harsh blow life had dealt them.

When the three of them arrived with the truck piled full, it was like welcoming old friends home. Becky immediately took to Maria, who went with her into the living room and turned on a kid's show before sitting on the couch with her. Becky took Maria's hand in hers, looked her in the eye, and then turned her focus to the TV.

Lisa turned back to Carla and Chris, who were standing there smiling. "She hardly ever takes to people right away. Is your mom Ok with her do you think?"

"Oh, she's in her glory now! Come on, I'll help you get unloaded and set up."

Together the three of them brought down the meager belongings that Carla and Chris could still call their own. They had a single bed for Becky, some boxes of household things, and an air mattress that the couple were sleeping on. Carla explained that the room they had been in was quite small, so they had been putting the air mattress up against the wall during the day time so there was some floor space for Becky to play.

Lisa also had them bring down the little table and chairs that were in the garage. It wasn't much, but it would be enough for them to be comfortable. Carla teared up again when she saw the balloons and flowers. "Becky's going to love them!"

After a quick check that Becky was still OK, Carla and Chris got her room set up before bringing her down. Maria slowly walked down the stairs with them, and Becky kept pace with her, one careful step at a time. When they got down the stairs and showed Becky her bedroom, it was clear she was happy with the arrangement. She gave Maria a hug, and then went and lay down on her bed, cuddling the teddy bear Carla had put on top of her pillow.

The adults turned back to the living space, and Lisa casually mentioned that there were some groceries there to get them started. This got Carla crying again, and she hugged Lisa and Maria before they went upstairs.

Maria settled into her chair in the living room while Lisa went to the kitchen to quickly put together a chicken caesar salad for supper. They were both quiet until Lisa brought over supper.

"What are you thinking?"

Lisa paused before answering, "It's like this whole journey has a purpose beyond us now. I was so focused on my own dream, and now suddenly the dream has expanded beyond my expectations. Their rent will still go towards my financial goals, so it's not like this is totally selfless, but I feel like giving them this space makes me feel far better than just finding good tenants."

Maria agreed. "Lisa, I know I keep saying this, but I'm so proud of you. You could have used your past as an excuse to be mean and selfish, and nobody would have blamed you. But instead, you just keep on doing good things for others. I have a beautiful safe home now, and Amy has a place where she can grieve, and then look to the future, and now Carla and Chris and Becky all have a safe place too. And it's because of you, and the smart decisions you've made."

Lisa looked over at her mom, "It's like we're all getting a chance for that transformation that Carrie was talking about! I can't wait to tell her about everything that's happened since she left this afternoon!"

Maria laughed, "I'll give you this, you sure can make things happen in a hurry!"

When Amy got home from her late shift, they filled her in on their big day. She was as happy as they were that there were good tenants downstairs and was looking forward to meeting the little family.

CHAPTER 41

When Carrie came over with her kids and a few pieces of framed artwork a few weeks later she noticed a difference in how the house felt. It was clear something special was going on that was more than paint and flooring. After exclaiming over Carrie's art, Maria chose a beautiful large one that framed a silk scarf in brilliant reds and oranges, and Lisa insisted on buying another print with soft colors for above her own bed. Then they sat down at the table, and Lisa told her about their new housemates.

"It's worked out so well to have them here! The week after they moved in, Carla got offered a full-time job at a supermarket. So when the bus brings Becky home from school in the afternoon, she stays up here with Mom until her parents are home. They pay mom for childcare, and Becky really loves her afternoons here."

"And how do you feel about the new arrangement?" Carrie asked Maria.

"Oh, I love it! Becky and I get along just fine, and it feels so good to know I'm helping them and earning a bit of money. I look forward to every afternoon. She's such a smart little girl, it's just that her language skills get in the way. I've been learning some sign language online using YouTube videos, and we're getting better at talking to each other!"

"Becky's way happier at school too," Matthew offered. "I can tell she likes to sit beside me, and she doesn't scream anymore like she used to sometimes. I heard her helper telling the teacher that she's doing really good."

"Well, kids can tell when their environment is stressful, or when their parents are stressed. I'm guessing now that Becky's here with people who love her, and she knows her parents are OK that she can relax when she's at school." Carrie looked at Maria, "But she's not the only one going through a transformation, is she?"

Maria smiled, "No, she's not. It's given me a purpose to my days."

"Plus, mom has taken over all the Airbnb stuff for the room we rent out! She handles all their inquiries and lets them in if I'm at work. Pretty much every review mentions how lovely she is. We're a straight five star Airbnb now!" Lisa was thrilled that her mom had taken over for her. They agreed that she would take 25% of the income in exchange for her work, so it was a win-win for them *and* their guests.

"Do you mind me asking how much it works out to in a month? I've been thinking about how that might help me pay a mortgage in the future."

"Well, we've only been doing it for about a month now," Lisa answered, "but it averages $250 a week. That's almost double what it would be for renting the room out by the month. I really like having that alongside the consistent income from renters. It's a good balance. And we've met so many interesting people already!"

"Definitely something to keep in mind, although I think I'm going to need a studio for my refinishing work before anything else. Those big picture frames were fantastic! I sold the ones that I've finished so far, and they really turned a nice profit."

"I wish I had more to offer you!"

"Well, I'm a regular at all the thrift stores now, which works out pretty good. And we're getting into yard sale season, so my Saturday mornings will be filled with adding more stock as we visit those. I figure I'll buy everything I can get my hands on now, and then when I go back to school I won't have to spend so much time looking for frames."

"The one you did for my room is just so beautiful. I think having a scarf framed instead of a painting gives it some texture and interest that sets it apart. You've got a great eye for how to put it all together!"

"Thanks Maria. It's something I really enjoy doing, so it's nice to know it's appreciated on the other end too!" Looking at her phone, Carrie noted it was time to go.

They said their goodbyes and promised to keep in touch. Lisa loved spending time with Carrie. She came across initially as quiet and gentle, but she had a strong, confident approach to everything and when she talked to you, she made you feel important and capable. If Lisa had a bigger place available, she'd give it to someone like Carrie for free so she could spend her time counseling people!

After Carrie left, Lisa spent some time working on the yard before going in to make supper. Chris insisted on taking over the lawn mowing, which gave her more time to trim back the extra growth, and plant flowers. The tulips were all up and blooming. They were like nothing Lisa had ever seen before. The petals were almost feathery and the colors were a variety of soft pastels, with whites and reds popping up here and there for contrast. She added annuals to the flower beds around the tulips, and her yard was becoming almost as nice as the neighbors.

The evening was spent finishing up on her freelance work for the week, and checking her finances. She had spent almost $5,000 in total for the basement development, but it added an extra $1,000 in income every month. Along with her freelancing and Airbnb income, she was saving over $2,000 per month after paying all her expenses. Keeping Janet's advice in mind about saving to pay taxes, she was putting $800 a month aside for taxes in a high interest savings account, $200 went into general savings, and the rest she put against her mortgage.

Sandra had secured a mortgage for her where there was no penalty in paying extra towards the principal every month. Lisa decided that one of her new financial goals was paying down her mortgage early. By the end of the summer she would owe less than $230,000 on the house. Frank came for a visit shortly after she had finished the upstairs renovations, and he felt the house was worth at least $400,000 with all the work Lisa had done.

But worth more than owning the house and paying down the mortgage was knowing she was responsible for giving a good home to her mom, her friend, Becky's family, and all the guests who stayed with them in the one Airbnb room. It felt like she had a good place in the world, and there was no price she could put on that feeling.

Plus, she had good people in her life now who helped her get where she was, and would continue to be there for her. Lisa decided to throw herself and Maria a housewarming party. They were well settled, and she wanted to say thank you to everyone.

In no time at all, she had ten people invited to come over the following Saturday afternoon for a little celebration. She begged Betsy to let her hire the aunts to cater it, and then her mom insisted on buying beverages, so in the end there wasn't much to do except buy paper plates and plastic cups for everyone!

On the day of the housewarming party, Lisa and Maria both had fun dressing in bright summer colors. Lisa had on a short, lime green wrap dress with a pair of matching sandals and her hair up in a high ponytail. Maria wore hot pink capris and a white sleeveless blouse. For now she was wearing white sneakers that she had to wear for support and balance, but both women were on the lookout for cute supportive shoes.

Lisa wandered through her friends—new and old—and enjoyed watching them get to know each other. She even invited Jesse, her mom's neighbor from the old house and he surprised her by agreeing to come. He was standing on the deck drinking a beer and paying very close attention to what Amy was saying. Lisa made a note to ask him over for supper one night when Amy wasn't working if they were still enjoying each other's company later!

Kara, the physician's assistant came with her husband Ken. Lisa told her to bring her kids too, but she laughed and said she wouldn't dare do that to Lisa. Ken was talking with Manuel about some mutual friends. Carrie had introduced Kara to Carla, and they were all talking together. Lisa smiled at how happy Carla looked. The dark circles under her eyes and the worry lines on her forehead were gone. She often thanked Lisa for giving them a place to stay, but Lisa felt like giving her mom time with Becky was the best gift.

Sandra and Frank were looking quite friendly too. They were having a conversation about the real estate market in the city, but Lisa thought there was an extra sparkle in Sandra's eye as she was talking. It would be nice for her to have someone around that could make her smile like that more often!

Becky was sitting on the floor with Matthew and Katie. She had brought some of her stuffed animals up, and it looked like Katie was setting up a tea party, while Matthew seemed to be interpreting Becky's gestures to Katie. The simple innocence of these three kids playing together despite their differences made Lisa feel a bit emotional. She walked into the living room where her mom and Janet were talking about her mom's favorite subject—Lisa.

"You know Mom, other people may not be quite as interested in talking about your daughter all the time," Lisa teased.

"That might be the case, but they're going to hear about it anyways!" she retorted.

Turning to Janet, Lisa asked how her dad was doing. "He's doing alright. I think we've got all the right people in place to help care for him. Some days are harder than others."

Maria put a hand on Janet's arm, "You've got a good heart, just like

Lisa. But Carrie told us how important it was to take breaks from caring for your parents. Maybe if you start, Lisa will finally take a break too!"

"I think it's easier said than done. But you're right. Even leaving to come here was hard, but now that I'm here I can already feel myself relaxing."

"That's the magic of this place! Even the Airbnb guests who are just here for a night or two talk about how relaxing it is to be here. And this summer Chris from downstairs is going to put in a deck area and a fire pit in the backyard for Lisa so we'll be able to sit out there in the evenings and relax some more."

The suggestion from Chris came just when Lisa was trying to figure out what to do with the backyard. She would supply the materials and he would do the labor. What he didn't know was that Lisa and Maria had also bought a playhouse kit to go in the backyard. It was specially designed for kids that needed accessible play areas and they knew Becky would love it.

People continued to visit well into the evening, and Lisa loved the feeling of love and friendship around her. The next weekend was the neighborhood BBQ, and she would get the chance to meet even more people, but the people here tonight would always have a special place in her heart. She wasn't sure what was next for her, but she was keeping her eyes open for the next challenge—and opportunity —to come her way.

A NOTE FROM THE AUTHOR

A Note From the Author:

Thank you for taking the time to read *The Cost of Caring*! If you enjoyed it, please consider telling your friends or posting a short review. Word of mouth is an author's best friend and much appreciated! Thank you again!

To be the first to hear when my next book comes out, and for a chance to win bookish prizes, sign-up for my newsletter:

www.carmenklassen.com

And you can like my Facebook author page:

fb.me/CarmenKlassen.Author

May all your days be full of good books, nice people, and happy endings.

Sincerely,

Carmen

READ ON FOR AN EXCLUSIVE SNEAK
PEAK OF BOOK 3...

"Matthew! Please!" Carrie tried to connect with her son, to somehow make him see that this was all wrong and that she loved him and his sister more than anything. But his steely glare didn't change. He started to pull Katie away.

"Katie-girl, you know I love you!" But Katie, too, couldn't be reached. She wasn't even looking at her mom. Instead she was turning towards her Dad—the man she had always been scared of— and getting ready to follow her brother into a dirty-looking van with dark windows.

"It's over now Carrie," Don sneered, his hand gripped tight on Matthew's shoulder. "I never forget when someone screws me over. Say goodbye to your precious little babies. When I'm done with them, they won't even remember you."

"NO!"

Carrie gasped as she woke up. Her heart was beating so hard it was causing her physical pain, and she felt like her spirit had been shattered into a thousand pieces. She looked over at Katie, worried she had cried out loud and woken her up. But Katie was still sound asleep in her bed next to the mattress Carrie slept on. Quickly Carrie slipped out of the room and went downstairs to her favorite armchair.

She wrapped a blanket around herself and tried to breathe deeply to calm her pounding heart, but every breath felt like it would crack her ribs. "What the heck?" she whispered as she looked up at the ceiling. This was the third nightmare in a row. In each one her ex-husband Don was taking her kids away—and the kids wanted to leave.

It made no sense. Why now? She was supposed to be happy! For the first time, she was making enough money to support herself and the kids. Don was in prison and still had another year to serve on a drunk driving conviction. The divorce was final, and she was starting grad school in September. Everything in her life was better than it had ever been. So why was she getting such terrible nightmares?

She didn't know how long she sat there, trying to reign in the panic her nightmare had created. Finally, she dragged herself up to bed, knowing sleep wouldn't come easily, and tomorrow she'd have to face the day and pretend that everything was fine…

ALSO BY CARMEN KLASSEN

SUCCESS ON HER TERMS

Book 1: Sweet, Smart, and Struggling

Book 2: The Cost of Caring

Book 3: Life Upcycled

Book 4: Heartwarming Designs

Book 5: A Roof Over Their Heads (Preorder)

* * *

NON FICTION

Love Your Clutter Away

Before Your Parents Move In

51212360R00139

Made in the USA
Lexington, KY
01 September 2019